PULP Literature

PULP

Literature

PULP LITERATURE PRESS

Issue No. 48, Autumn 2025

Publisher: Pulp Literature Press; Editor-in-Chief: Jennifer Landels; Acquisitions Editor: Mel Anastasiou; Senior Editor: Sierra Louie; Poetry Editors: Daniel Cowper & Emily Osborne; Copy Editor: Amanda Bidnall; Proofreader: Sierra Louie; Graphic Design: Amanda Bidnall & Sierra Louie; Cover Design: Kate Landels; Subscriptions: Carol McCauley; Advertising: Jared Schellenberg; First Readers: Amber Allen, Mark Cameron, Michaela Chan, Summer Keown, Sylvia Leong, Tara King. For advertising rates, direct inquiries to info@pulpliterature.com.

Cover painting, *Selfie* by Akem. Illustrations for 'If I Could Hide Away Anywhere' by Sierra Louie. All other illustrations by Mel Anastasiou.

Pulp Literature: ISSN 2292-2164 (Print), ISSN 2292-2172 (Digital), Issue No. 48, Autumn 2025.

Published quarterly by Pulp Literature Press, 21955 16 Ave, Langley, BC, Canada V2Z 1K5, pulpliterature.com, at $18.00 per copy. Annual subscription $60.00 in Canada, $80.00 in continental USA, $92.00 elsewhere. Printed in Surrey, BC, Canada, by Fraser Printers Ltd. Copyright © 2025 Pulp Literature Press. All stories and works of art copyright © 2025 their authors as per bylines.

Pulp Literature Press is based in the unceded traditional Coast Salish Territories of the Katzie, Kwantlen, Matsqui, and Semiahmoo First Nations.

Pulp Literature Press gratefully acknowledges the support of the Canada Council for the Arts and the Government of Canada.

Pulp Literature is a proud member of the Magazine Association of BC and Magazines Canada.

TABLE OF CONTENTS

FROM THE PULP LIT PULPIT

On a summer's day in 2013, founding editors Jen, Mel, and Sue had drained our glasses when the alliterative question arose: *Sould* Pulp Literature *publish poetry?* We knew we'd need a brilliant published poet with a gift for editing, and Mel said, *What if I ask Daniel?*

Daniel Cowper is a beautiful poet who spent seasons in Toronto with the iconic Algonquin Square Table. He said yes, thank goodness, and began to create a superb poetry collection for the quarterly. He supported Canadian and international poetry communities, and also conceived of the Magpie Award for Poetry.

A few years in, when Daniel was much published and winning prizes for his work, he met Dr Emily Osborne helping out at a soup kitchen. Emily's specialty at Cambridge was ancient Norse literature, and by the time they married, she was publishing translations and writing poetry that won awards as well. She joined Daniel as editor and brought her own brilliance to *Pulp Literature*. Their bibliographies grew, as did their family, and throughout they continued to make time somehow to edit *Pulp Literature*'s poetry and to long- and shortlist our poetry contests. Frankly, with their own careers and busy family life, we don't know how they did it.

Talent shines, we know. We will miss their work on *Pulp*'s poetry. We're excited for their new directions in family life, working life, and publishing across Canada and internationally.

We welcome Sierra Louie as our new poetry editor. Sierra's editing work on *PRISM international* attracted notice and admiration from staff and writers, and we're excited that she's agreed to take over this essential section of the quarterly.

Thanks again, Daniel Cowper and Emily Osborne! Look for Emily's forthcoming collection, *The Skalds*, in 2 o 2 6 from Norton Publishing, and Daniel's newest book, *Kingdom of the Clock: A Novel in Verse* (2 o 2 5), from McGill-Queen's University Press.

Read and be happy!

~ *Mel Anastasiou*

*I*N THIS ISSUE

Follow cover artist **Akem**'s *Selfie* into myth and mystery with 'The Tales of Fanon and Gavroche' by feature author **Renée Sarojini Saklikar**.

Make connections over seemingly impossible gulfs with 'Downwelling' by **D Marmara** and 'M4RINR' by **Mike Carson**, and discover what the night-time holds in **Mel Anastasiou**'s 'Moonlight Over Paradise Gardens' and Part 4 of 'Their Grandfather's Chair' by **JM Landels**.

Fly away with a gorgeous mischief of three very different Magpies by **Pattie Palmer-Baker**, **Angela Rebrec**, and **Elizabeth Cockle**, and then come home to nest with **Sierra Louie**'s elfin adventurer in 'If I Could Hide Away Anywhere'.

Have a stiff drink with **Melissa Ren** at 'The Midnight Diyu', or pick a potion with **Lena Ng** in 'The Curse of the Chattering Skull', while you mingle uncomfortably with strangers in **Mitchell Toews**'s 'The Light Pool' and **William Kitcher**'s 'I Can't Tell You That'.

THE TALES OF FANON AND GAVROCHE

Renée Sarojini Saklikar

Renée Sarojini Saklikar *is the author of five books, including the award-winning* Children of Air India *and* Listening to the Bees. *Her essays and short fiction have appeared in literary magazines and anthologies, including* Exile Editions, Chatelaine, The Capilano Review, *and* Pulp Literature. *She was Poet Laureate for the City of Surrey (2015–2018), co-founded Lunch Poems at SFU, and teaches creative writing at Douglas College.* Bramah's Discovery, *the third volume of her epic fantasy in verse series,* THOT J BAP, *is forthcoming in 2026 with Nightwood Editions. She lives in East Vancouver. 'The Tales of Fanon and Gavroche' is a work in progress, excerpted from* Bramah's Discovery.

The Tales of Fanon and Gavroche

♛ ♛ ♛

A note from the author

In ***Bramah's Discovery***, the year is 2110 and Bramah's journey, to discover the truth about her origins and to find out more about her parents, continues. Along the way, this time-travelling locksmith must rescue her friend Amahl the Beggar, who is trapped in the Eternal Game of Climate Chess. She eludes an evil drug lord; encounters two shape-shifting mythical beasts, Fanon and Gavroche; breaks free from captivity in Baghdad; and engages in a battle of wits with a Paris collective of supernaturals. Each challenge forces Bramah to discover truths about her own demigoddess self, and about the price of idealism in the face of ecological and economic calamity. *Bramah's Discovery* is forthcoming with Nightwood Editions in the spring of 2026.

Thank you, *Pulp Literature* magazine, for welcoming readers to the shadowy lands of Consortium, an integrated global economic and administrative empire covering most of the known world and controlling all aspects of industry, agriculture, and food production. Accelerated climate change disrupts the supply lines and access to electricity and scarce fuel resources, collectively known as the Big E. These are crucial to Consortium as its power weakens. Locations include Pacifica, a reimagined North American west coast, with towns and cities collectively controlled by Consortium and known as Perimeter.

Dramatis Personae

Bramah — the elusive time-travelling locksmith on the hunt for the beggar boy, Amahl;

Amahl — trapped into playing the **Eternal Game of Climate Chess** by Consortium;

Fanon and Gavroche — two shape-shifting mythical beasts who represent, simultaneously, a number of ephemeral conditions caused by accelerating climate change. They were once seasons, April and October, and can now shapeshift into beasts whose existence Consortium attempts to deny;

Al Rashid — a pseudonym for an underworld drug lord and known double agent of the Consortium who undertakes various clandestine operations such as kidnapping, exhortation, blackmail, and the control of orphan children. No one knows his real name;

Two **Guards** of Consortium's infamous networked chain of detention centres known the world over as Detention Centre C;

T-LOHK (the Last of Her Kind) — an itinerant scribe, providing services to record eyewitness sightings of mythical beasts and supernaturals. Consortium will sometimes hire T-LOHK as a night clerk because of staff shortages;

Abisha, the Oracle — beloved by street children, Abisha is deft in the arts of disguise: seed saver and textile worker, debonair sword warrior, old crone. Abisha supports Bramah's quest to find Amahl the Beggar;

Shall we begin?

<u>Transcript Number</u>: protected information
<u>Delivery</u>: street sweepers brigade, Section A, Perimeter Zone P
<u>Production</u>: Night clerk: 'T-LOHK'
<u>Method</u>: Parchment scrolls, inscribed
<u>Video Surveillance Log</u>: currently unavailable
<u>Source Citation</u>: textile worker
<u>Name</u>: Abisha
<u>Transport Permit No.</u>: data unrecoverable

One night, waylaid by Guards — and I let them, you understand? — I wanted to see if there'd been word left for me at my usual spot, a scarred oak bench deep inside the Snuggery. Built tongue and groove, the tavern once thrived on the edge of Perimeter, where the Good-Bye river snaked its way left then right to the ocean. Now the bricks and mortar sagged over the bridge, where the river, more often than not, ran as a mere trickle, spring freshet memories receding. The taproom floor caught sawdust into the folds of my saree, and migrants lined up for hours, drinks in hand. They came for miles to get a scribe to write their stories, messages, letters to far-flung family members indentured or on transport shifts. Every now and then, especially at the new moon or just after a full waxing, those eager to share a sighting would jostle for the front of the line. Each time that happened, they'd swear, "Listen, could be Bramah herself, so keep it secret, keep it safe!" And the scribe would look up, face without expression. The barter: extra scrolls of parchment, homemade quills, small pots of ink. Once sprinkled with sawdust and dried, these scrolls sometimes came my way — never ask me how!

In those days we'd hear street urchins chanting words about the lost seasons: brown hands begging in dusty alleyways; orphans, huddled in culverts exposed by all the rubble, bombed streets, torn concrete. Rumours swirled that these lost seasons were changelings, shape-shifting into mythic creatures. Throughout the hidden valley, you could hear voices echoing clear up to Settlers' Hall deep inside Perimeter.

> *Calendars to count, seasons one to four*
> *Un coup de dés, jamais, jamais*
> *Twist, pull, turn the lock, Bramah with your key*
> *Winter, spring, summer, fall—*

It was only much later, after the fifth catastrophe, with water companies bankrupt and Al Rashid's armed gangs patrolling the valley, that a group of these children showed themselves to me.

Of course, they were on the run; rumour had it they supplied Bramah herself with digi-codes to unlock Seed Vault treasures hoarded by Consortium executives. And it was the children who told me the story of that first shape-shifting seasonal encounter: two beasts, large and cat-like, slinking through the electric gates, vault to hall and back. Although my eyebrows rose, my lips resisted smirking. In those days, all things rich and strange had a habit of reoccurring. The children sang to me of Bramah:

Come, Bramah, give this world a second glance:
what will you gamble to save those you love?
Roll the dice, never think twice, grab your chance —
calendars, tapestries, twist, twill, and pull!
   Threads or pages, walls or clocks —
    find Settlers' Hall,
you'll find power for all!
     Jump the fence, throw the dice
      Move your queen
      Protect her twice —
    Un coup de dés!

Then they said, "Aunty Abisha, look here, see these lines, rub this parchment."

The sing-song gaiety in their voices dropped quiet, and they gathered round me, shoulders lifted against any possible drone-watchers. Those drones! They'd whizz and whine in no time, it seemed, anywhere we seed savers gathered.

Here is what the children found: a parchment letter written in the faintest India ink.

"These inscriptions!" My voice quavered to touch the words, knowing the children could not read. They smiled, gap-toothed, unheeding my words. They just wanted to see magic happen.

"Rub, Aunty, rub."

They always loved to touch the lettering found on cast-off papers, old documents, and especially treasured, parchment: this one embossed with an antique ivory chess queen. My hands trembled. I knew it was special as soon as I read the inscribed words, repeating in low tones what the migrant had said: "Could be Bramah herself!"

♛ ♛ ♛

Scroll #1, as found by *Aunty Abisha, seed saver, at the Checkmate Tavern.*

I was told to hold vigil before dawn
my forehead clammy with sweat, hands shaking —

Tanacetum parthenium, I heard voices say:
blood platelets eased; smooth muscle spasms stopped.

I saw in the far distance, two seasons shifting:
April and October, felines purring,

one white as a daisy, with yellow eyes;
the other a tabby burnt-grey and black:

they transformed yet again into Siamese
once-white kittens, now their colour points, dark.

In the palm of one cat: a dozen leaves,
take only one or your mouth will blister.

I obeyed and lay down in the tall weeds;
my companions with me amid feathery chamomile,

spindly stems, yellow centred, parsley frayed.
When I woke, my fingers, as if grazing cement walls:

Images shimmered into view. Both cats rubbed my arms—
    None other than my beggar boy!
locked tight in a room he could only cry:
Bramah, come save me and turn your key fast

At his plaintive story, those two cats just smiled:
we've saved you, now tell us about this boy—

As I read these words, the children clamoured around me, crying, "Aunty, Aunty, look here, there's more!" I peered into their small brown hands clutching dusty rolled remnants of khadi-cotton, ripped silk, stained and faded. Looking over our shoulders, we stepped deeper into the shadows. I waved my left hand and a small gold light glowed. The children shrieked with delight and then dropped to their knees in the dust. A drone sped by. They were too busy crouching to notice the drone didn't spot me at all. When it passed, I read out the second parchment.

Scroll #2, April and October: Fanon and Gavroche

Feline, they mimicked each other,
sodden spring air, in the gloaming, whiskers quivering:
full-heavy-wet-flesh buds pushed past brown leaves.

Lush or withered, full or empty, bookends
marked by quiet paws, mist or fog;
long lidded, with patience to wait, then prowl

damp soil, rustles in the grass, chilly nights.
Nostrils intent on scent, tails raised to pounce
rip-nip-tuck, shake, tear, side to side. Neat heads

curling sun dappled, their own book of hours,
each equinox apportioned to their stare:
slow blinking, cherry orchard or full moon.

Purr and prowl they slipped through borders and gates
in between spaces, air to iron bars
cells in the Secret Centre, oak boxes

stacked six by six high. Haunches tensed
and jumped, tails flicking, silent landings,
eyes glittered in the dark, they knew to watch—

Said Fanon to Gavroche, morn, night
Tidy your home, shake out your welcome mat.

Said Gavroche to Fanon, *sweep your hearth*
When the north wind blows, polish your urns clean.

Cat to cat, they meowed, no one to understand:
coal embers, stirred, stoked, fires burning bright.
They laughed, coughing: *Find a man who stays true,*

plump up your pillows, look under your bed.
Sou'-easters rattling, you'll sing to the dead

Look to the moon, her pull — and push right down
unleavened bread, hot cloths, toes to the ground;

cut back your long hair and keep your lips soft.
Linden to Banyan, stay high in their loft

Count out your coins, and bury your hatchets.
If trouble's a racket, carry your matches —

Fanon and Gavroche, they sang of themselves
*   never tarry without us, turn and seasons end,*
when fall turns frosty, when winter's reach releases
spring's first days, not quite vernal
find us in our cosplay,
sing us, Fanon and Gavroche.
They'd alight ahead, hind legs on edges of space,
Detention Centre surveillance, dividing lines between
    errands, missions, mercenaries of weather change.

        . . .

Purring deep in their throats,
Fanon the first to jump into any cell, line-up, interroga-
tion rooms
    lightning quick, doors open, adjacent
corridors, where prisoners squatted under watch

        . . .

Gavroche always second, followed by Fanon's echo,
I'm Sykes so call me marked, their calls, loud;

À bientôt! replied Gavroche, a zephyr blowing east,
holy places scratched
and released.

Outsiders would hear only the caterwauling.
Fanon laughed and coughed up a hair ball.
Gavroche swore moon-oaths and sang,
    Come ye, Aunty Pandy!
Fanon said, *No one talks about that anymore.*
  Gavroche said, *Your heart's all crooked,*
    your heart's a cold whore; Aunty Pandy,
      you'll never catch me.
  Fanon sighed, stretched their claws and said,
    The likes of we, oh all right then,
    jumped the fence, you should too!

♛ ♛ ♛

I made sure that spring and fall to find my way to the White Queen Assembly Depot, Factory Zone A. In those days, workers lounged at break time outside the massive wrought-iron and concrete walls. Armed overseers at the outskirts of the demarcation square, on a site outside Perimeter's walls, allowed a certain measure of ingress, especially if we brought them cigars, so rare. Better than young children for the factory floor. I hated that and found my little ways and means. A flick of the wrist transformed children into will-o'-the-wisps. Then, of course, the challenge was to remember to trace my path back to the spot and re-engineer … Well, never mind. Some days were better than others. I did my level best. I had my own mission, to seek news about Amahl. Instead, I heard again about those shape-shifting beasts. And there appeared, as I knew it must, out at the far end of the depot gates, a single battered oak table and, seated behind it once again, a scribe. And again, a long line of workers on their break, eager to have someone write for them. One young woman, red skirt, hair black as jet. Was there a rose tucked behind her ear? I cannot recall. In any case, eyes darting to the Guards, she shoved into my hands a long set of scrolls wrapped tight, one within the other.

♛ ♛ ♛

Scrolls #3–5, as tucked into Abisha's saree by the textile worker, red skirt a flash of colour outside the White Queen Depot, Factory Zone A.

When Bramah spied them, they snarled and hissed.
Of course, she tamed them with tales of magic,
   shared secrets and travellers' gossip
      Ahmedabad to Baghdad
      Paris to Pacifica.
Bramah said, *Letter to necklace, chalice to book;*
fragments of parchment, old floppy discs,
saved; oak box buried up by the old well,
weeds grown over; Hidden Valley safe.
Gavroche rubbed against her thighs, sly and sleek,
   Come, Bramah, hurry, else we'll have to tell——
      Fanon sang with a scratch and a soft purr,
Ever-shrinking ice floes, oceans too warm
   yes, yes, let the white queen rest.
Bramah stared at Fanon, then Gavroche.

Climate chess! It's a terrible game, she said, *once started, betrayal sure to follow!*

At the sound of Bramah's voice, both Fanon and Gavroche sat upright on their hind legs, front paws soldier straight, tails curled, eyes wide. Both creatures still, their whiskers quivering, they listened.

Bramah Remembers Fighting Al-Rashid

All alone in his Secret Centre, he'd call
or send signals transmitting through time
ribbons cut, leather pouch open, rubies
spilling, where at dusk six sails curved past—

Once she met him face to face, his eyes flicked
blank, staring her body up and down; he lounged,
his lanky length cold and yet supple,
no give to his arms, sinewy muscles.

She heard his tuneless whistle and soft song:
    Once you walked, Bramah, under fir and oak.
    Bramah shuddered at these words.
    Once you were a princess longing for home.
    Bramah resolved, shed not one tear.
    Memory an oak tree, charred stump, forest road.

Scythe at his side, unobtrusive advance
their underground meeting, battle-ready flash!
Wielded blade first, sharp arc ambidextrous

force to mow down, slice, sudden scoops, blood spurts
Never felt a thing, she'd say afterwards.

Worse though when he'd plunge, release, to linger
days, weeks, months, his poison hard to evade.
Bramah knew to stop, step aside, careful
senses primed to watch. That stench, rich, rotted
how to be ready, his grey cloak dragged dust
      face hidden, rank breath.
Once, she recalled, flash memory, dodging thrusts
      Aunties laughed and said,
        When that Angel comes for you
          just tell him to—
Bramah would not say the word.
She thought it, though. And smiled.
   Light-footed, quick with her key and lock.
And did she fool that warrior, him with his cloak,
      sharp-sided scythe?
Yes, she did, at least for a while.
She persuaded him to take a drink,
up at a settler manor house, tapestries once faded,
      vibrantly alive with mossy greens,
        radiant golden threads.
Pacifica in the very last days of the Before. And then—

Bramah shook her head free of her memory-place.
Instead, she smiled again:
   Images danced before her closed eyes.
   Two shape-shifting seasons, April and October.
     Under the right spells, they'd transform

into four-legged creatures.
It were Bramah who in the end named them:
Fanon and Gavroche
        two immortal prized cats,
        season to animals,
when the world turned fresh and temperate,
now in the employ of Al-Rashid;
as long as he paid them with access to
        Portals, Gates, Seasons: time's telescope pulled —
            pounce, strike, devour, Fanon's tail to twitch twice.
                Ever-shrinking ice floes, oceans too warm
            Fanon sang with a scratch and a soft purr,
                dirges for Gavroche, whiskers quivering —
                    yes, yes, let the white queen rest.
        Eyes to stare round, then blinking
            just the right amount of purr —
cheese, mice, or anklebone, slinking through bars
            cell to cell in the Secret Centre
whiskers quivered in the dark before paws tugged,
            claws tucked; actions timed to steal
            or to aid escape.
First light to sunrise;
sunset to the last;
where sky meets earth,
azure bowl cut in half.

In time this song became the Song of Fanon.
        And Al-Rashid would laugh and grin, and say,
            Never call me wretched!

It were Bramah, gathering all places
every wind blowing, every city wall
inscribed, engraved, painted: slogans and dates
Queens, kings, knights, bishops
roses and wine: a thousand scented nights
silk, gold, rubies, strands of pearls, copper clasped
in the hands of Harun-al-Rashid, jesting —
she spurned him with her wiles, beat him at chess.

She taunted him as the Caliph al-Raqqa.
Bramah, he begged her, *just one more story:*
Why not a thousand and one, she whispered?
Her flashing eyes, her smooth plaited hair unravelling.
Unhurried, the great Shah smiled, his cold glinting eyes.
And did Bramah sense danger? She did.

And did Bramah hear beneath her feet,
trapped in miles-thick granite
the hoarse cries of the beggar boy,
chained to chess, eternal game?
Each move to stave off East Antarctic melts,
his wrists and tendons throbbed, calf muscles ached.

Years later, Bramah would say,
Each word a barbed wire swallowed whole:
Don't think for a moment I found the Caliph attractive.
It was the game, the chance, the risk, sharp energy
    flowed within.
Then she'd tug her hair into one long plait. And close her eyes.

Scroll #4, Fanon the Cat's *Shape-Shifting Song About How They Met Bramah*

Let me tell you, once a shapeshifter—
always a-changing, that's how we get to nine lives,
season to creature,
    faster the change, quicker our shift
fare forward voyagers, forward and back—
yes, I was that indentured snow skater
sent to spy on children by the evil Al-Rashid,
yes, he's that bad, him with his eternal game
climate chess, forward, back, across, falling
    leaves; mist rising,
        lick and purr
        scratch and post
—born in April, I learned to shift, winter calling.

Ice-pink parka, lambswool muffler, fluffy mittens.
Snow-boots laced knee high, heels with rubber
treads, crunching against train tracks, cheeks rosy
spread into smiling when they came for me
click, click that silence in the plane, transport:
my head heavy, hands shaking, eyes blurry.

Another time they came for me through walls
cracked, paint flaking, ants racing, tap-tapping
louder and louder until I fainted and woke
I did not know the place,
blinded in a labyrinth, only to trace words.
How could I fathom meaning without light?

Unchained into spring, released, I fell face
forward into green, Consortium's lawn:
One robin pulled worms and faint sounds echoed.
Notes playing on a piano; cream-coloured
walls embedded with cameras: point swivel —

. . .

Who will ever believe how I was made?

Here's my Tale of How I First Met Bramah:

Scroll #5, Fanon the Cat, *Who Used To Be April, Sings a Song of Meeting*
Bramah

Outside that hall, snowflakes falling, she stood
silent witness, her bare arms felt no cold
I'd slunk to the rafters of an old smelters' hall:

Up there in Pacifica, the year 2 1 0 9
   I heard a vagabond sing,
Calumet, Calumet. No one heard.

Bramah, eyes closed, inhaled frosted air.
Then wide open her sight, year after year:

copper and tin, ores mixed or malachite.
Red Sea hills, turquoise and emeralds traded.

Syria to Egypt, desert routes trekked.
At the sign of the Ankh, Cadiz in Spain,

from her sandal strap, a loop crossed over
Nile to Euphrates vessel, rod, bracelet.

Those shafts dug deep, waterwheels turning.
Chrysocolla, cried child workers, knees bent.

Greenish blue their lips, soft and sooty hands.
Accidental metal, sulphur, iron slags.

Women at the forge, hard hammering, hot
tongs to soften, tin added to the melt.

Come, Bramah, cried the children side by side:
You — be our copper, you make us your bronze.

Then Fanon the Cat Told Bramah:

I wept to hear these beggar children.
I asked if they'd heard of a chess player,
Have you seen a boy; their name is Amahl?
I smiled and nodded as their small heads circled,
now yes, then no, then yes, chanting in Gujarati
thirty days hath September
no one left to remember
Bramah find the Secret Centre!
Travel west, you'll know best,
bruised bodies bent from day labour
chipped yet striking teeth,

white in brown dirty skin.
Dust-covered, they paused,
arms lifted, brows furrowed,
they asked, *What is November?*
Who is left to tell?
Their voices raised in laughter,
rolling sounds, words on their tongues,
only the hot, only the dry;
came the wet, turned freezing cold.
Oh, Bara Dari, twelve doors, three sides,
Oh, bring us the seasons, flowing inside.
Another child cried out, *Who has seen the wind,*
and another, the smallest, with a gap-toothed grin,
replied, *I have! Grabbed their tail, quick as a wink*
    their name was Gavroche!

. . .

    They found written at the bottom of a page:
        abandoned black notebook, Paris café.
        No one left to remember the other names
        Seasons fled through the last of the Portals
        Only two cats slinking past city gates.
    Yes, of course, it were me and Gavroche.
    But I mustn't speak of them. It is too sad a tale.
        Instead, listen to this one, the Tale of the Fire Gilders.

Transcript unavailable. Follow the spring release!

§

For more short fiction and verse from Renée Sarojini Saklikar, check out 'Man with Golden Helmet' in Pulp Literature *Issue 28, Autumn 2020, and 'Told Under the Linden Tree', a Bramah side tale featuring Ciswen the Blacksmith, in Issue 37, Winter 2023.*

FEATURE INTERVIEW

Renée Sarojini Saklikar

Pulp Literature: *'The Tales of Fanon and Gavroche' is an excerpt from what is now the third instalment in your series The Heart of This Journey Bears All Patterns (THOT J BAP). With* Bramah's Discovery *forthcoming from Nightwood Editions in 2026, what have you discovered about this saga of yours, and its many characters, since writing your previous book,* Bramah's Quest *(2023)?*

Renée Sarojini Saklikar: As a poet known often for my experimental poetics and avant-garde tendencies, a key discovery in writing epic fantasy is the discovery of how much I *love* world building, seeding my poetry with fantasy elements, merging the verse with novel-like structures. Along the over ten-year journey of this world building and character making, I've also discovered the energy that comes with staying open to the sometimes subtle and slant visitations from characters. For instance, the hero-anti-hero, Bramah, first came to me on a long-ago bus ride from UBC to East Vancouver; just a passing view of a small bronze horse on a verandah filled with knick-knacks, in a ramshackle house glimpsed down East 41st. As well, another key discovery: how hard it is to write plot and develop structure, as well as craft poems, all at the same time. Truly, it's a challenge, and one that I hope has helped me grow as a writer. A colleague of mine, commenting on my body of work, gave me feedback recently that I've been processing: they see each of my books as 'absorptive', from delving into the tragedy of Air India Flight 182, to working with a world-renowned honeybee scientist, to embarking on this epic saga, THOTJBAP. Throughout it all, I've learned to just stay open to musings, however diaphanous, dreamy, or mystical. Doing so seems to lead me to characters I fall in love with … That helps to keep going!

PL: *The THOT J BAP series, described as an epic fantasy saga in verse, is so striking in its use of form. This most recent excerpt is especially intertextual, incorporating transcripts, scrolls, and songs from within the story world itself. When populating such a rich world with poetry, oral history, and all manner of inscription, how do you decide when to stop? Surely you could go on creating stories within stories forever.*

RSS: The story and the characters usually speak up and let me know what is needed. That's if I give myself time and space to listen to my work: if, as writers, we can get out of the way of the poem, the story, the novel, things just seem to go better. And, yes, that ancient epic device beloved of Scheherazade, the nested story within a story, is seductive!

PL: *Like those that came before, this story grapples with a range of ecological and economic crises. If readers were to leave this story with one grand takeaway, what would you hope that might be?*

RSS: In the face of unprecedented economic uncertainty and our current climate emergency, how can we, as individuals and as communities, find and practise hope against all odds? As

Bramah's motto states, *Let All Evil Die and The Good Endure.* How do we each interpret that?

I guess in my books in this series, I'm ultimately grappling with that question and hope the characters and the tale(s) will plant seeds in the reader to do the same.

PL: *When working on an immersive, long-form project such as the THOT J BAP series, do you ever find yourself itching to work on other things? What do you do when you discover your mind wandering elsewhere?*

RSS: Yes! All the time. I've been blessed with my connection to *Pulp Literature* because I have a place to work on the 'spin-offs' that branch out from the main books. As well, as a practice point, I do keep an elaborate set of notebooks to capture other ideas: snippets of poetry, usually a sound pattern or image. And my iPhone, it must be said, comes in super handy. I will often use voice memo to save those 'itchings', if you will, 'cause you never know when or how your creative impulses might take form and shape. Save everything!

PL: *The last story of yours that we published was 'Told Under the Linden Tree' back in Issue 37, Winter 2023. Outside of the THOT J BAP series, could you share what you have been working on since we last spoke with you?*

RSS: A few things: I am deeply moved to be collaborating with health sciences professionals to create a work in progress that deals with nurses' experiences during Covid-19. As well, I continue to work on a children's story, *Mystery and the Bee Locket,* for which I was honoured to receive a Canada Council grant. And I'm in the very early stages of a creative non-fiction work, the working title of which is 'Sarees, Sermons, Settlers', about my family's diaspora from India and across Canada to New Westminster, BC, where I did a lot of my growing up. I now teach at Douglas College, so it's interesting to contemplate departures 'from' and arriving 'back to' migrations.

Select Bibliography

Renée Sarojini Saklikar is the author of five books, including the award-winning *Children of Air India* and *Listening to the Bees*. Her essays and short fiction have appeared in literary magazines and anthologies, including *Exile Editions, Chatelaine, The Capilano Review,* and *Pulp Literature*. She was Poet Laureate for the City of Surrey (2015–2018), cofounded Lunch Poems at SFU, and teaches Creative Writing at Douglas College. *Bramah's Discovery* is the third volume of her epic fantasy-in-verse series, THOTJBAP. She lives in East Vancouver.

THE EXTRA TAKES THE CASTLE: A MONUMENT STUDIOS MYSTERY

Mel Anastasiou

Mel Anastasiou writes the Fairmount Manor Mysteries, the Monument Studios Mysteries, and the Hertfordshire Pub Mysteries, available at pulpliterature.com. She won a Literary Titan Gold Book Award and was longlisted for the Leacock Memorial Medal for Humour for her novel Stella Ryman and the Fairmount Manor Mysteries. Look for Stella Ryman and the Search for Thelma Hu, available through online booksellers and at Pulp Literature Press.

Frankie Ray's acting chops and investigative talents have taken her far from her Vancouver home and set her on what she hopes to be a path to success in the movies. But 1930s Hollywood seems to have little regard for a presently blackballed, though still registered, extra. Now employed in the star-studded Castello Hotel, Frankie's friendly encounter with a famous director, and rumours of a screenplay any producer would kill for, are all she needs to raise her hopes and send her sleuthing after this fabled prize.

The Extra Takes the Castle, Part 2: Moonlight over Paradise Gardens

Frankie Ray hung up her chambermaid uniform in the Castello Hotel closet and donned the chic pointed hat that she shared with several other movie extras. This first day might have been the longest and hardest an unemployed actress had ever worked outside a movie studio. However, the rumour of screen pioneer GX Forrest's hidden treasure — a long-lost, perfect screenplay — and her unexpected encounter with the most important director in Hollywood ensured that she'd be back on the morrow.

Would director Des McMann remember Frankie after their afternoon tracking the hotel fire up to GX Forrest's apartment? A regular person would, but he was not that. She could only hope. And, as an extra blackballed from the Monument Studios lot, she was good at hoping.

Frankie was adjusting the dashing angle of the hat in the reflection of the elevator doors when they opened to reveal the director himself, Des McMann. He flapped into the foyer in his bedroom slippers and called her by name.

"Frankie Ray! I'm off to bed." Resplendent in a red velvet robe over yellow striped pyjamas, McMann yawned and ran his fingers through his hair so that it stood up comically. "Come see me tomorrow morning, will you?"

Frankie clasped her hands in front of her. "Yes, sir. What time?"

"Come up when I've had my coffee?"

"Yes, sir."

"I will have pots and pots of coffee. A fellow at Schwabb's delivers it with my morning grapefruit and jar of mimosa."

"What's mimosa?"

Des McMann laughed. "It's a kind of southern breakfast porridge. Leave me now and I'll see you tomorrow, once my body is refreshed by sleep and my humanity restored."

"You're human as anything, Mr McMann," Frankie assured him. She pushed the elevator call button, and he flapped back inside and up towards his apartment on the third floor.

Frankie drew a deep breath of appreciation for the great man's friendly attitude to a chambermaid. After all, she had spent her day at the hotel covering for the rest of the young staff, all of them absconded from their jobs and off to the studios to work in the movies. Fooling her gosh-awful manager was satisfying, but there was no disguising the fact that cleaning commodes and dust was not the ideal way to advance her acting career. She grimaced at the thought and then grimaced at the grimace, for you didn't see Marietta Valdes, the great star and hopeful director, wearing her thoughts on her beautiful face. If Frankie was going to be an actress, which she darn well was, she must learn to control her features. It was something she'd be smart to practise during her exile from the studios. That, and her Marietta Valdes walk.

She touched a hand to her hat, grateful for its hauteur and for the platinum hair beneath it that showed no dark roots. Then, confident as an unemployed actress could be, she set out along Sunset Boulevard towards Monument Studios. She reminded herself that although King Samson had banned her from his studios, not even he could stop her from gazing upon his studios with ambitious eyes. Nor could he prevent her from walking like a movie star.

She placed her feet with care, not straight out from the hip as her physical education teachers had taught her, but left foot directly in front of right, and right directly in front of left. Athletic girls like Frankie enjoyed a good stride, and she'd witnessed Marietta's barefoot tomboy walk in the star's unguarded moments, but a proper, glamorous swing of hip and swirl of skirt must become another string for Frankie's bow. All along Sunset, she improved her form and increased her pace until she reached Monument Studios' enormous twin gates. She sashayed past the empty kiosk where Dickie, the genial and intransigent guard, had more than once stopped her from entering. Tonight, she imagined the studio gates opening and the director of *The Emperor of New York*, with his black coat and unloving gaze, gesturing her inside. This was not a likely outcome, but neither was it impossible. Those gates might swing wide someday, and she might swagger inside and onto set, just like Marietta Valdes.

Tonight, the gates didn't open, but the small door set into them banged wide, and two shadowed figures pushed through it and closed it behind them. A tall woman with an armful of what might have been metal tubing was followed by a slender male figure carrying a box. Frankie took a step back. She wasn't sure how best to handle a night-time encounter with two mysterious figures absconding with armfuls of loot from a movie studio. Traditionally, one ran away from robbers, and Frankie was set to go until a searchlight swung across the sky and, in its gleam, she recognized the pair.

Marietta Valdes walked in the lead, barefoot and splendidly beautiful; she clasped a long, folded tripod to her breast. At her heels trailed Leo Samson, King Samson's understated son, holding a large black box. He wore an expression of pain and regret. Frankie well knew that the pain resulted from a healing gunshot wound to his shoulder. The regret was no doubt because he'd listened to Marietta and gone along with whatever mad, ambitious plan had brought them here.

Leo whispered, "Frankie?"

"*It is I,*" the former schoolteacher replied. "What a pretty night, don't you think?"

The two stopped and shifted their burdens.

Marietta said, "Francesca Ray. You owe me a favour."

Frankie did owe Marietta a favour, since she'd rescued her from certain death. However, as Frankie had saved the movie star as well, she felt that honours were about even, although she was not about to score points against a woman at the top.

"Yes, of course," Frankie said. "Leo, what's in the box? You should put it down before you tear that wound open."

Leo put it down. "It's a — "

Marietta interrupted. "You must swear secrecy, Frankie."

"I swear."

"You must swear to help."

"Er, I can help you and Leo carry things."

"And you must swear to support our great endeavour in any fashion I consider necessary."

Frankie didn't swear to this one, and she arranged her features into a listening, open expression to hide her resistance to any of Marietta's more outlandish schemes. "Here, Leo, let me take half the weight of whatever that is."

"It's a camera," Leo said. "One of my dad's old movie cameras."

The box looked far too small to carry Leo's usual movie camera and paraphernalia, but Frankie knew Leo well enough to believe him. She wrapped her arms around the box. "Rest your hurt shoulder. Where are you going?"

Marietta shoved the tripod into Leo's empty arms. "I'm going back in while I can, to get a director's chair."

"You are what you sit in," Frankie said.

"Write that down, Leo," Marietta said. "Anything snappy anybody says, write it down."

"My hands are full," Leo said.

"Carry a notebook. You'll get screenwriting credit for interesting dialogue. And I need a screenwriter." Marietta slipped back through the door in the studio gates.

Certainly, Leo's mother, the gossip columnist Blanche Carver, carried a notebook wherever she went, and she ruled Hollywood with what she wrote in it. Frankie decided to buy a notebook at the five and dime. An actress had to hold herself ready for any sort of entrée to acting in the movies.

"Marietta will catch us up." Leo shifted the tripod in his arms. "Let's go before she makes us carry the director's chair as well."

"How far do I have to carry this box?" Frankie asked.

"Just to Paradise Villas, to my place." Leo had the bungalow next to Frankie and Connie's. "Lead the way."

Frankie headed back along Sunset towards home. She dropped her movie star walk in favour of a more practical slog, for the box in her arms was an awkward burden. "What do you need a camera for, anyway? Your father lets you use his anytime you want. And pays you."

"He has good equipment, too. Third-best cameras go to me if I'm in his good books." Leo sounded gloomy, but that was Leo for you. "The most you can say about the camera you're carrying is that nobody will miss it."

"Is it small because it's old-fashioned?"

"Old-fashioned like an Egyptian mummy."

Marietta, barefoot and carrying a folded-up director's chair, padded up behind them. "It's not the camera that's important. It's the composition, the architecture of the shot, and the landscape as portrait through the prism of the artist's eye."

"And stealing the right kind of film," Frankie guessed. "That's another kind of expertise, I'll bet."

"Remember to write that down, Leo," Marietta said. "Now, come along, both of you."

The star pushed up front and led the way along Sunset. Her steps never flagged, and she moved as if the director's chair in her arms weighed nothing. Frankie shifted the camera in its box as she walked, and Leo puffed along behind.

Frankie asked, "Why are we stealing a camera?"

"Borrowing the camera," Leo said.

"Liberating a camera to work," Marietta said. "It's an old machine, but it's still capable of great things. Additionally, King Samson is too preoccupied with his next film to notice that it's missing."

Marietta used to call King Samson *Sammy*, and the change told Frankie all she needed to know about the breakdown of romance between the two leading figures at Monument Studios.

"Then, you and Leo are making your own movie?"

"Yes," Leo said.

"No. First, we're making our own studio, and then we'll make a movie," Marietta said. "I won't serve another minute as Samson's peasant. I will not for another second remain the shine on his boots and the dirt beneath his heel. I want my chance to direct and produce, and I want it now, while I've got my youth and my energy and Leo here as an underappreciated, third-rank cameraman."

"Dad said I was gaining experience," Leo explained. "But Marietta is right: I'm ready to head a department."

"A department of one," Marietta said. "But that's how all the great studios began. Think of DW Griffith's early work, camera to hand and the little Gish sisters under his thumb."

"My mom once asked the Gishes about their hard lives as child actors," Leo added, "but they insisted they loved every minute." Leo's mother Blanche Carver was not only the top Hollywood columnist for *The Los Angeles Morning Gazette*, but she also owned Paradise Gardens. "And the man who used this camera worked alone with it well past the aughts and into the war: the great GX Forrest himself, rest his soul."

"But he's not dead. I actually met—"

"Great work like his lives on, Frankie," Marietta broke in. "Forrest and Griffith began this town. But they didn't finish it. They waited, diminishing in power and projects, for the great studios to call them back and set them to work."

"Marietta doesn't wait," Leo added.

Marietta continued, "Griffith is hardly a memory, and GX Forrest died long ago, his last screenplay buried with him."

Frankie shook her head. "Well, everybody thinks that GX Forrest is dead, but I actually met him, and the rumour of his great unproduced screenplay—"

"If it was as good as he said, he'd have produced it and died in his glory," Marietta said.

"But he's not dead——"

"Don't interrupt," Marietta, the greatest of all interrupters, told Frankie. "Learn. As with the giants of the past, it all starts with a camera. The camera and the director's eye."

Leo said, "*And* the cinematographer's understanding of the powers and limits of the lens and film stock."

Frankie gave up. At least Marietta was informative, and she had apparently put new life into Leo. "Oh! You're a cinematographer now. That's admirable."

"Marietta says I always was." The pride in Leo's tone made Frankie smile.

Marietta said, "Once a cinematographer's eye has seen, it can't unsee."

By now Frankie had become so interested in the conversation, imagining its inclusion someday in a 'how they got their first break' article in *Screenplay* magazine, that she was startled to find herself walking under the *Paradise Gardens* sign into the crowded klatsch of rented bungalows she called home. Marietta raised the director's chair over her head to pass along the narrow brick walks leading through the duplex bungalows to Villa 7A. Frankie and Leo set down their burdens just inside the door, and Marietta sent the two back outside onto the front stoop with a directorial gesture.

Frankie cocked her head at Leo. "But that's your house."

"Sure it is."

"I don't think you should let her kick you out of your own home, Leo."

"She's the studio head, though. I'm just the cameraman."

"You're the cinematographer, and you're the one who's going to interpret Marietta's grand vision in a film that will make the audience swoon."

"Swoon?"

"Yes. And critics will find new words for beauty," Frankie insisted.

"My goodness." Leo shook his head. "Hard to imagine, isn't it?"

Not to Frankie. Always hopeful and ever can-do, to her the idea of a studio beginning in a low-rent bungalow, equipped with one camera, and led by an actress-turned-director in a world not just designed but staffed and funded by men like King Samson, sounded like a proposition that deserved to succeed against all expectation.

"Talent, spit, and elbow grease," Frankie said. "And look, here you are, a cinematographer in a brand-new studio."

"I ought to feel like a million bucks, but instead I feel like I skipped a step getting here," Leo said. "I don't know whether indulging my big ambition is tempting fate."

"Gosh. It's the only way, Leo, if you want to walk the path of the mighty."

Leo squared his shoulders and stepped back inside Villa 7A.

Alone on the stoop, Frankie smiled up at the sky. Everybody had to start somewhere. She remembered King Samson's words the night she'd first met him.* His own beginnings hadn't been propitious: *Up in a two-room walk-up, I had a wife who was waiting with a hot dinner for me, and a nice kid. I was a free man. I had a happy little life. Then the Great War came, and somebody handed me a camera instead of a gun. So here I am. But would I go back? Would I?*

―――――――――――

* See the Monument Studios Mysteries, Book 1: *The Extra*.

King Samson hadn't answered his own question, and he didn't need to. Frankie understood why he pushed forward, even when the past looked green and easy, like an unending picnic on the banks of a slow-moving river. That was not a life a mover like Samson could tolerate. Nor did it attract Frankie. She nodded up at the North Star overhead, long a guide to travellers. The North Star had it right: *Never go back. Never give up.* She'd had the luck, good and bad, to meet a few of the notables in Hollywood over the last few weeks. The greats were all wildly at odds in their approaches to their work, but alike in determination and persistence.

And what did determination and persistence have in common?

They didn't cost a dime. The aptly starry sky above was the limit. It was just that she couldn't see a clear path to get *up there* from *down here*. But others had found a way.

Frankie adjusted her excellent hat, turned on her heel, and hurried back to Villa 7A. She knocked on Leo's front door and stepped past him into the little living room. Its tiny kitchen opened to one side; its bathroom door stood shut, as did the door to Leo's bedroom where she'd recently spent a long night on the run from the police and a murder charge. Before her, Marietta Valdes, Hollywood's newest and greenest studio head, sat at Leo's dining table and scribbled in a lined school notebook.

Frankie said, "Marietta, you're going to need an actress."

"I've got an actress."

The bathroom door opened, and Connie stepped out. She stopped short when she saw Frankie. "Hail, hail, the gang's all here."

"Good for you, Connie." Frankie turned back to Marietta. "I'd like to join, too, if I may."

Marietta folded her arms. "Leave your name with my secretary."

Frankie looked around the little living room. "Where is your secretary?"

"My studio hasn't hired one yet."

Leo said, "Then how can she leave her name?"

"It's a problem," Marietta admitted. "But it's not my problem. Please see Frankie Ray to the door, Miss Mooney."

Connie opened the door for Frankie and the two stepped outside. Connie said, "Look at that, Marietta remembered your name. That's a shiny start to stepping into her studio. *Posi-lutely.*"

"*Abso-tively.*" Frankie tried to sound confident. "Well, at least it looks like you're in."

"And I'll work on getting you hired, too. Meantime, I haven't seen any sign of money, and there's no contract for me to sign, so dollars to doughnuts I'll be out on my ear the second she can hire somebody bigger than me. But who knows? She'll need smaller folks to kick around, too."

Frankie nodded. "And you're extremely photogenic." She didn't bring up the sore subject of Connie freezing up when the camera focused on her. But Frankie's best friend would be able to practise acting, because before Marietta could start filming, she must somehow find investors, editors, writers, best boys, makeup artists, lighting directors, set designers, and all the other employees that a studio head had to employ and pay before she could become a powerful scoundrel and bully like King Samson. And, if she liked, Marietta had time to invent her own Hollywood as she went along, just as GX Forrest had done back in his day, before the war.

GX Forrest. The name reminded her that Marietta Valdes's new film studio was not the only showstopper for the day.

"Listen, Connie," she said. "While you and the rest of the Castello staff were working at the studios, something big happened."

"I know! The attic fire," Connie said. "What a drama for the Castello Hotel! And remember the fire on the set, that time when I almost died?"**

As a substitute teacher back home in Vancouver, Frankie had exercised some self-control over sarcastic retorts, so she only replied, "The Castello fire was the least of today's occurrences."

"No. I met …" Frankie discovered that she didn't yet want to mention her afternoon with Des McMann. "… I met GX Forrest."

"Ah." Connie nodded her understanding, which was good acting on her part.

"GX Forrest was one of the great directors when the movie business was starting out."

"So? I mean, besides bowing to legends, it doesn't sound like a big event—not like meeting Clark Gable, say. Can GX Forrest help?"

"He is not a helping kind of fellow."

"Not a kind kind of fellow?"

Frankie resolved anew to write down clever lines like *kind kind* for Marietta Valdes. "No. But a giant. And, the thing is, he once wrote a screenplay that was the best of its kind. And it was never produced. *And* people want it."

"What people?"

Frankie raised her eyebrows and gave the moment a beat. "Producers. Directors. People who can help you, me, and the other kids get ahead."

** See Book 1: *The Extra*

Connie didn't have to act comprehension this time. "I wish we could buy it. And then we could star in it."

"Nobody can buy it because nobody knows where it is. But if somebody found it . . . ?"

"Somebody smart? Somebody who is maybe good at sleuthing?"

"Don't overestimate my powers. But I'll try to find it."

"This is an excellent plan." Connie's smile was the brightest it had been since the two Vancouverites had stolen Frankie's father's car and run away to Hollywood.

Frankie said, "Don't tell anybody, of course."

Connie's eyes widened. "How can you say that, when you told me?"

"Knowing something like this is like keeping mad money in your pocket. You don't take it out until you're sure it's time to spend it."

"But we help the other extras, too?"

Frankie nodded. "It's like you said: when one of us gets ahead, we help everybody else. I want to find that screenplay."

"And then offer it to Marietta Valdes, to get into her studio?"

"Maybe."

And what of King Samson and Des McMann, giants of the studio? How far could she get with them if she had the screenplay?

Both questions made her feel uncomfortable, as if her father, the defrocked minister, was looking over her shoulder. Sheridan D Ray wouldn't pull his verbal punches. She heard his voice, with all its stertorous power, say, *Greed, daughter! Fear it! For it is an open mouth and a closed heart.*

Frankie checked her heart and saw what greed had caused her to forget: the author of the perfect screenplay. She would have to persuade GX Forrest and his wife Lillian to sell it, and she'd have to come up with a darned good reason for them to change ten years' stubborn refusal to do so. But that was a question for another day. Sufficient for now was the mystery: Where was it?

The sound of table legs dragged across the brick patio and the crack of a match on gasoline-dampened sticks in the oil-can barbecue heralded Paradise Gardens' nightly get-together. Connie joined the extras around the barbecue, and Frankie hurried into Villa 7B, where she took off the lovely hat to pass on to the next girl who needed it for a job interview or a date. Out of the icebox, she took the enormous bowl of potato salad she and Connie had thrown together the night before. The ice in the box was a quarter the size it had been when the iceman had brought it the week before, but the salad was cool enough for confidence. Indeed, there was truth in Connie's boast that nobody had yet died from their cooking.

Frankie delivered the potato salad to the patio and returned to 7B to fetch the bungalow's two rickety chairs. She had to duck under the string of parrot-shaped lights Doris and another extra were hanging across the dancing space. Tom helped steady the tables. He was still made up from his day as a female extra in King Samson's film *The Emperor of New York*, on the very set Frankie had been cast out of earlier that day. The thought should have pricked her like a hatpin, but under the warm lights, greeting the young extras bearing bags of bread and cases of records to play, she felt no sting of failure. She was an extra still by virtue of this all-encompassing friendship; it was possible that she was an extra forever, or at any rate for as long as she and Connie lived here. And Marietta? Funny thing. Although she shared Hollywood with Frankie and the other extras, and had taken over Leo's bungalow for her office, a movie star would never truly belong in Paradise Gardens.

To nobody's surprise, Tom set himself in place to control the gramophone output, and the jazz number 'Cocktails for Two' buzzed and leaped its way around the increasingly crowded patio and up into the indigo night. Paradise Gardens folks began to dance, quickstepping around the barbecue and calling out for favourite tunes. 'June in January' and, most often, 'The Continental', which never failed to make Frankie blue for the two minutes and twenty seconds it took to play, recalling as it did a recent night of doomed romance, dancing, and gunfire.*** But her mood was snapped short by a shout from Villa IA, followed by a bumptious procession of extras carrying the round-back cane chair where the Queen of the Extras sat in her flowing black robes. Not long out of hospital, Loretta Desirée had that day removed the bandages from her head and draped the shaved spot with a lace mantilla. On her nose sat Frankie's sunglasses, which Loretta had been instructed to wear day and night to save her sight after her operation. She loved wearing the sunglasses, and Frankie was so happy to see the Queen, back in her rightful position at the centre of all their fun, that she didn't care much if she ever got them back.

The extras set their leader down with care. Loretta's spot was where it had always been in Frankie's experience — next to the table with the gramophone and records stacked on top and underneath. 'The Continental' arrived at its scratchy conclusion, and Frankie cheered up further still when Loretta Desirée, Queen of the Extras, got to her feet and raised a hand for attention.

————————————

*** See Book I: *The Extra*.

She didn't have to ask twice. All dancing stopped as snappily as if a director had shouted *cut and print*.

"My dear children, here we are, all together again."

Whooping answered her, and she smiled the mysterious smile that had kept her in black robes and rent money since her vamp days in the silent pictures twenty years before.

Tom said, "What's your pleasure, my queen?"

"I would like to hear 'The Continental' again…"

Frankie's shoulders slumped.

"… and I would be most grateful if you would cook and distribute these."

From somewhere inside her robes she produced several large oily packets wrapped in brown paper and tied with string. Tom pulled off the paper to reveal ropes of linked sausages, and Frankie ran to help Doris set them to cook on the blackened grate that topped the oil-drum barbecue.

Doris caught sight of the potato salad. She put her hands on her hips. "This is not sliced bread. This is not sausages. How in blue heaven are we meant to eat potato salad?"

Frankie blinked. She hadn't thought of cutlery. She and Connie owned only two forks, and that was their sugar spoon in the potato salad bowl.

Connie appeared between Frankie and Doris. "Eat it with our fingers!"

"Eat it with our toes!" Tom countered.

"Lick it off the plate!"

The queen raised both hands. "Everyone must bring their own fork and a plate."

"They'll leave them in a mess," Doris said.

"So what?" Tom asked.

"There! You heard him. Tom will clean it up."

"Tom won't," Tom said. "Tom lives off his own cutlery."

Loretta Desirée spoke. "They will take their cutlery home. I have seen it in a dream. Also, there's a big call-out for you all to Monument Studios in the morning."

But not for Frankie. Still, tomorrow beckoned. And tonight, the stars shone down while around her the extras argued over how charred the sausages should be for perfection in grilling. The evening air was summery, although it was only early May. Growing up in Vancouver, she'd appreciated the frequent sound of spring rain on rooftops because it meant she wouldn't have to hang out laundry or sweep the stoop. But now that Frankie — this was the only proper word for it — *resided* in Hollywood, it was clear she hadn't known what she was missing. California's reliable clear skies worked to cheer her hopes and calm her professional worries. She had a hatful of each.

The gramophone crackled its way into 'Swing, You Cats'; the extras danced until the sausages were blackened and ate until the food was gone. Music piped up again, and, true to Doris's prophecy, the extras tossed their plates and forks into the gardens around the patio area. It seemed an even bet whether the extras would take them home when the dancing ended or the ants would have the time of their lives.

§

For more Hollywood adventures with Frankie, pick up a copy of The Extra: A Monument Studios Mystery *by Mel Anastasiou, available from Pulp Literature Press and most bookstores.*

THE LIGHT POOL

Mitchell Toews

Mitchell Toews *is a Canadian writer with a strong periodical publishing and literary contest history. His collection of short stories,* Pinching Zwieback *(At Bay Press, 2023), was met with widespread critical acclaim and earned a place on several bestseller lists. A novel in the author's gritty style, revisiting themes like belonging and overcoming adversity, is forthcoming in 2026. His work can be found in* Pulp Literature *issues 20, 27, and 38. A longer version of this story first appeared in 2016 in the Spanish-language publication* Lingo. *It was presented in Spanish and formal Ogden Basic English as a language learning tool for the site's online subscribers. Mitch and his wife, Janice, live in the boreal forest where they "drink deeply of the wild air."*

The Light Pool

I was in Toronto for training with my boss, Maddox Jarvis. She was a rising leader in the company, favoured for the Western Canadian Director position. Originally from Toronto, she suggested I accompany her to a party that evening. "I'll introduce you to a few friends. We'll have a drink and leave early."

The low house was distanced from the street and shone like a ship at sea as we crossed the baize lawn, close-mown and fragrant. Guests, I supposed, were old-money chums from this stone-fence neighbourhood in exclusive Rosedale. I was an awkward outlier to this clique — a young rustic from a backwater somewhere out west. As the evening progressed and the beer I had insisted on bringing sat unopened, the long knives came out. ("Look, everyone, a six-pack!")

My many small social miscues accumulated, and I felt like Tarzan in the Royal Albert Hall — a mildly entertaining distraction.

My urge to push back finally won out, and I didn't care if I confirmed their conceits. *Were they condescending snobs, or was I just too brittle?* Either way, I let old resentments steer me and became abrasive. I was saved from challenging the whole living room to a fight only by their growing lack of interest. Maddox watched me while she caught up with her friends. Her nervous hands spun an empty wine glass on the table in front of her as I burned my bridges, if not hers.

An attractive woman named Taylor made neutral conversation with me not long after I started my retaliation. She spoke to me quietly and looked into my eyes as I answered her questions. I felt unexpectedly befriended by one of those I was insulting. Maddox kept her distance, watching but avoiding my gaze.

A few minutes later, Taylor found me again and asked if I needed a ride; my hotel was on her way home. I looked at Maddox, who mouthed, *See you*, and shouldered her purse.

As I stepped into the car, I expected meaningless small talk. Uncertain, I waited for Taylor's lead.

"You know, you misread the circumstances."

I sniffed and looked down at my phone.

"Seriously," she continued. "We were teasing Maddox because she had warned us not to make you feel uncomfortable." She swung her hair and gave me a frank stare as we passed under a row of blue-tinted streetlights. "We would've backed off, but you can hardly blame us for continuing. You asked for it."

I opened the window and listened to the crickets and frogs calling from the valley below as the silver sedan crossed the Don River Bridge. Inhaling, I expected to smell fresh summertime vegetation—ferns and flowering trees. Instead, there was the vile stench of hog rendering and the reek of poultry effluent. I pushed the button and the glass hummed, nesting in the thick rubber rim.

"Maddox is my oldest and best friend. She's an open book. No pretensions. We all love her. Her family is the most powerful one in our circle, but you'd never know it, right? She is a substantial person," Taylor said, putting emphasis on the last words.

I agreed silently, thinking about how she had advanced my status at work.

"No one in that crowd tonight — except her — is going to have a second thought about you. It's not an issue for us," she said, looking over at me, the city lights shining in her face. "You should apologize to her. She didn't deserve the runaway train you became."

Taylor pulled to the curb next to a streetlight. Several dozen large beetles had gathered in the pool of light beneath it. The insects crawled on the pavement towards the bright centre, advancing in syncopated unison. Some paused to consume the squashed pulpy remainders of their kin: victims to passing cars.

"I'm turning off at the next intersection. Your hotel is three blocks up the street." She took a breath and added, "I'm not saying we're not snobs. But you are too. You give yourself credit for some kind of down-home depth of character and the whole salt-of-the-earth thing. Meanwhile, we are nothing but born-on-third-base losers."

I studied her profile in the street's sodium glow. "You're right about me ..."

After a pause, I proved her point. "Want to have a last drink to discuss it a little more?"

"Oh!" She touched her lips, then flicked the wipers on to bat a beetle off the windshield. "Yes, sure ... Maddox said you were a quick study."

THE CURSE OF THE CHATTERING SKULL

Lena Ng

Lena Ng roams the dimensions of Toronto, Canada, and is a monster-hunting member of the Horror Writers Association. She has curiosities published in weighty tomes including Amazing Stories. Under an Autumn Moon *is her short story collection.*

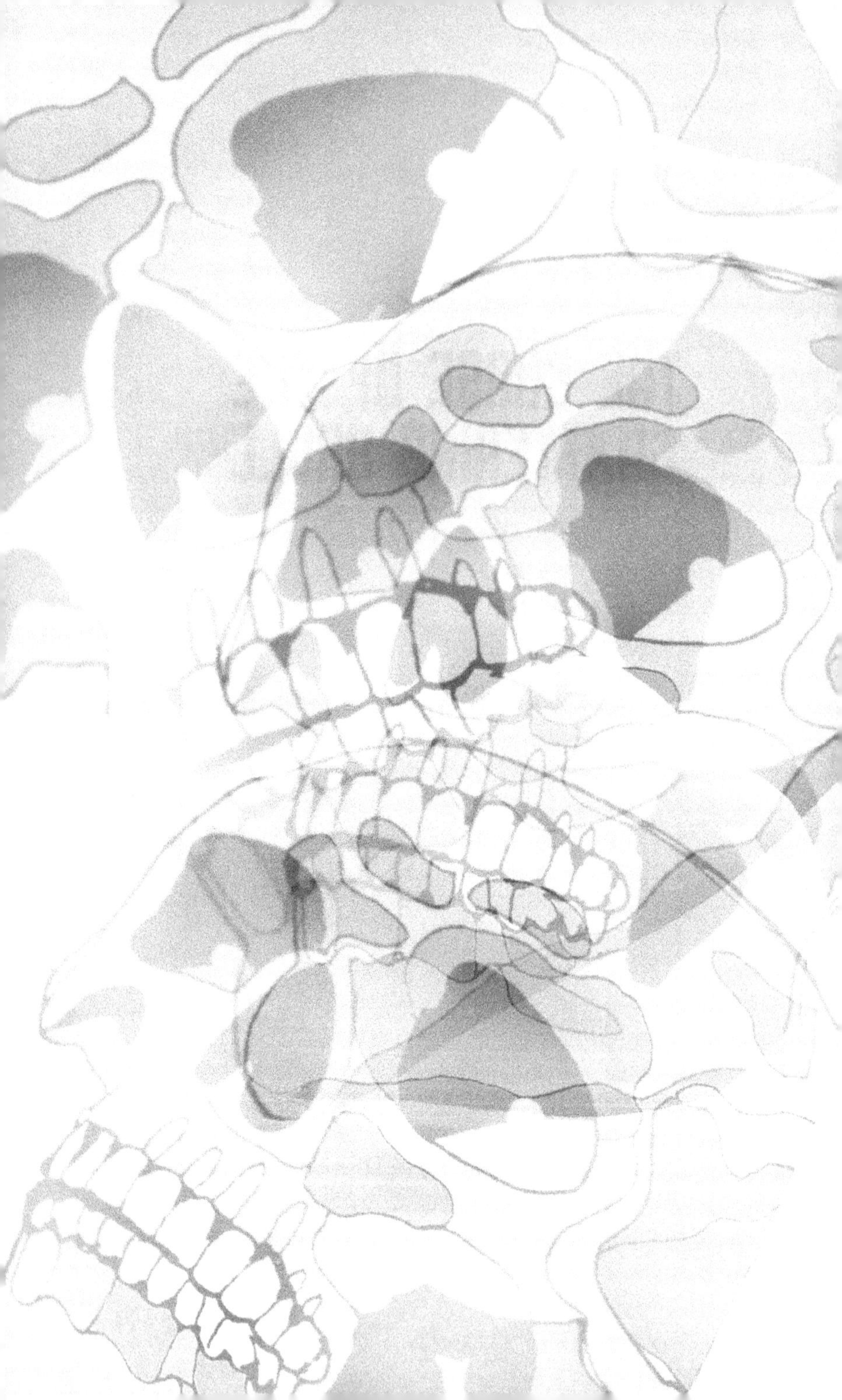

$\mathcal{T}$HE CURSE OF THE CHATTERING SKULL

I stirred the pot, waited ten heartbeats, and added the newt's eyelashes. A large purple bubble formed in the centre of the brew then popped, indicating that the potion was done. "That's better. There's no way it can't work this time."

I reached into the glass bowl. "Come here, Lucian." Gently, I pulled out the bullfrog. "Soon, you'll turn back into a handsome prince. I hope you'll accept my apologies for how long it took."

I grabbed a yew-wood teaspoon and dipped it into the pot. Lucian obligingly sipped it and gave a small belch. I looked at him, and he looked at me.

Nothing else happened.

Lucian croaked, exasperated. I promised I'd change him back. I was trying, really. But I wasn't the swiftest wand in the spellbox, as my mom always said. I was persistent, however, and there were only 7 6 9 8 combinations of the spell to go. "We'll try again tomorrow. Meanwhile, I've caught you your favourite: lantern beetles."

Lucian looked at me begrudgingly as he gobbled up the offering. Secretly, I thought he enjoyed being a frog. In fact, he was getting a lot of pressure from his father to create a war plan to invade the neighbouring kingdom, whose princess he had a crush on, so he had come to me for a shape-shifting spell. Obviously, that worked; it was the restoration spell I hadn't mastered yet.

I was taking inventory when I heard a tentative knock on the spell-infused door. I didn't have office hours since I needed all the business I could get. I had failed my licensing finals three times so hadn't yet joined the Guild of Magical Practitioners, but my prices reflected that, and those who came to me came at their risk.

The young man standing at my doorstep was dressed like a barbarian, but he didn't exactly look the part. His sword drooped from his loincloth, and his leather tunic was too loose around his frame. I had more muscle than he did, and the heaviest thing I had to pick up was a spellbook.

"Miss Esmeralda? Esmeralda Tanglewood?"

"How can I help you?" I unrolled the list of the spells I was close to mastering. "Love spells, cursive, hair taming, boss persuasion—"

"It's not that, it's …" He glanced around to confirm his privacy. "I need some herbal tonics to help me bulk up. I'm Damcor, by the way."

"Diet and old-fashioned exercise didn't help?"

"Tried that, but still skinny as a stick. I need some help if I am to become a barbarian."

He looked like he should be tallying up the gold coins in the King's treasure house, not swinging a sword. "No offence, but why do you want to be a barbarian?"

Damcor sat on the bearskin chair. "My father was a barbarian, and my grandfather. Heck, even my sister is a barbarian. She doesn't let me live that down."

I flipped through my spellbook. "What would *you* like to do?"

"Write poems. Unfortunately, the quill may be mightier, but the sword pays better."

I could see why his father wanted him to go into the trades. It was costly to keep ale in the mug and boar in the pot. "Why don't you hire a Guild magician?"

"I can't afford a Guild witch. I only have poetry money. Can you try?"

I couldn't afford to turn down a job either. I sighed and pulled out a consent form. "Sign here, and here, and here."

Over the next few days, I spent some time in the Spellaversity of Lower Arghull, doing research. I went to the market to gather the necessary ingredients. Lastly, I picked up a second hand skull cup to give the potion serving a professional air.

Damcor sat waiting, looking like his dream was about to come true. I slowly poured the potion into the skull cup. Just as he was about to pick it up —

"Aaahhh! It burns, it burns!" The skull cup rocked and tipped over, spilling the potion.

"That spell wasn't for you, it was for him," I scolded.

The skull clacked its jaws. "What would you expect from a second-rate witch?"

I glared into its empty sockets. "You'd better be careful or I'll sink you into a swamp."

The skull cackled. "That's all you got? You can't kill me, I'm already dead. And whatever little reputation you have will die when this gets out." It swivelled towards Damcor. "And what are you? A barnacle who wants to be a barbarian?"

The skull was right, but I was mad. I might not have been the best witch in the world, but I was definitely practising. I shot it with a silencing spell.

It hooted. "Good going, granny guts. My goldfish is a better witch than you."

I tried a reversal spell, a muzzling charm, and a mute potion. I tried a hushing concoction, a quiet tonic, and a gagging tea.

Finally—

SLAM. Damcor had picked up his sword and smashed the skull. He stared at the blade in wonder.

His father was right. Sometimes the sword was mightier than the quill.

DOWNWELLING

D Marmara

D Marmara was born and reared in the midwestern USA and now lives in southern California. She has an affinity for science, horror, and the macabre. Her work can be found in Xanax Hamster, Cosmic Horror Monthly, and Arkham Institutions. A former researcher, she now works in laboratory safety.

Downwelling

It was a German soldier who pulled Peter Corbin from the cold grip of the Atlantic. The U-boat had sunk the USS *Valor* in spectacular fashion, upending her stern to the Sargasso skies while the crew fled for the lifeboats. Peter wound up in a boat with his lieutenant, a man named Horace Radcliffe, and two privates. They'd taken to the oars to get clear of the wreckage as Radcliffe barked orders.

As the lifeboat turned west, Peter caught sight of the lurking, titan bulk of the U-boat where it wallowed in the seaweed-brown water like the grim Leviathan. In the changing light of the afternoon, he saw the glint of a periscope. Moments later, the guns struck the first of the lifeboats.

Pandemonium ensued. He heard the shouts and screams of the other men. Hulls shattered under ballistic fire. Radcliffe shouted something which was lost in the sound of the explosions, a bare moment before their boat was struck.

The concussive force sent Peter reeling. Light and sound, like the sun itself, screamed. The boat cracked like an egg, and they were in the water.

The cold ripped a gasp from him, and Peter wound up with a mouthful of seawater. He struck out, trying to get clear of the wreckage, to escape the tangles of sargassum. His life vest jerked him about the waves like a bobbing cork.

"Lieutenant!" he shouted, and received no answer.

Blood and bodies were in the water. Around him, limbs thrashed and drowning faces gaped in fishlike terror. The guns thundered, undercut by the screams of the dying and the silence of the dead. The ocean soaked his uniform, though he knew the good woollen fabric would stave off hypothermia. Though the water would surely destroy Cassie's last letter in his pocket, the one he hadn't had time to read.

The thought was agony, but he had no time to wallow in it. He swam. The current washed him in the direction of the U-boat, a mercy and a terror both. The arcing rainbows of gunfire were aimed well outward, but he feared he might be crushed against the menacing hull and sucked beneath it.

Figures stood on the deck, blurred impressionist paintings of German uniforms against the glaring sun. A man lifted a revolver. The crack of shot, and a projectile struck the water beside him. The soldiers spoke amongst themselves, then one man unhooked something from the deck and heaved it out into the waves.

It landed near Peter with an audible smack. A life preserver, attached to a rope. He stared at it, his veins iced with dread, as it bobbed in innocent fashion on the waves. What options did the Germans offer? Surrender and be taken prisoner? Escape the water to be granted the mercy of a bullet?

He could hear the screams and shouting of broken men. A deep, terrifying awareness of the icy, abyssal depths beneath his struggling legs, a starless expanse as vast as deep space engulfed him. Suffocated by shame, he grabbed for the life preserver.

They towed him without speed or care, leaving him to wallow and choke beneath the waves. He wondered if they meant to drag him thus forever, until he expired from chill and exhaustion. Perhaps they would submerge their vessel and drag him to his doom.

Instead they wrenched Peter from the water like a drowned cat. A gaggle of soldiers surrounded him. A man with an officer's bars cocked a revolver and pointed it.

Peter held his trembling hands above his head as they stripped his life vest and rifled through his pockets. The old soldier who'd grabbed him relieved Peter of his pistol, then kicked him in the thigh.

"On your feet, Ami," he said. A word Peter recognized: *American.* "You're going below deck."

One of the soldiers shouted, and the others turned to look. Port side, they were hauling something from the water. A comrade? Peter's spirits lifted. He struggled to gain a vantage point. Then he saw the limp limbs, cloaked in tangled sargassum, and the lifeless visage of Lieutenant Radcliffe.

He watched, helpless, as they inspected the body. One of the soldiers rifled through Radcliffe's bag. He said something to an officer, then held up a curious object.

It appeared to be a small carven figure, pallid as porcelain in the sunlight. The soldier rotated the object, and Peter caught a glimpse of coiled shapes, something which put him in mind of an octopus, or a centipede, or both at once. Dark holes formed a dozen eyes, like the carbuncle pattern of a spider's face.

A shiver gripped him. Lieutenant Radcliffe had been carrying that? He'd never seen anything like it.

The officer took the object and motioned to the soldier to toss the body overboard. The man obeyed, and Peter could only watch as Radcliffe slipped back into the embrace of the waves.

The old soldier shoved at his shoulder, and Peter moved towards the hatch. As he passed the railing, he risked a final glance at the choppy water.

Horace's body floated amid the sargassum, anchored to the surface by his life vest. His limbs flopped on the tide, dead eyes open and fixed upon the sky.

Yet in the moment before Radcliffe's corpse vanished, it seemed to Peter he saw those eyes move.

Then they were below deck, and he could not be certain. He stumbled into the depths, blinded by the sudden absence of sunlight. His eyes adjusted as the soldier marched him towards the aft end of the submarine, past the engine room and into the darkened cave of the crew's quarters. The lighting here had failed at some point, and the only illumination came from the door in the watertight bulkhead that separated the quarters from the rest of the ship. The light cut an eerie yellow slash across the floor and cast the majority of the room in shadow.

The man snapped a cold metal cuff around Peter's wrist. The other end went around a section of the bunk frame, leaving Peter chained like a dog.

"Stay put, Ami," said the soldier. Then the bulkhead slammed shut and left him in darkness.

The endless dark unnerved him, to know his eyes were open and yet see nothing. He listened, but could hear only the inexorable groan of the submarine.

"Goddamnit," he said.

"I suppose that's one way of putting it."

Peter jumped, brought up short by the chain. "Who's there?"

"I am," said the voice. A man's, by the sound of it.

"Are you another prisoner?"

"I suppose you could say that."

"You sound like an American. Were you on the *Valor*?"

"The ship? Yes, I was."

"I'm Sergeant Peter Corbin, out of Providence, Rhode Island. What's your name and rank?"

"My what?"

"Name and rank."

"I don't remember."

"Were you injured in the attack?"

"No."

"Then why wouldn't you remember?"

"I don't know what to tell you."

"Who's your commanding officer?"

"Does it matter?"

"Do you know what they're planning for us?"

"No."

"Have they questioned you?"

"No."

"Did they leave us anything to eat or drink?"

"There's a canteen under your bunk."

Peter felt around, found a strap. He braced the canteen on his chest with his forearm and worked the cork one-handed.

The first taste of water was ambrosia, but Peter tried to control himself. A thought occurred to him. "Did they leave you water as well?"

"Me?"

"Yes, of course."

"No."

"Why didn't you say so?" He swung the canteen by its strap in a tentative arc. "Have some."

Someone caught the canteen and lifted it from his grip. "You want me to drink this?" said the man.

"Obviously. Are you not thirsty?"

"Only rarely."

"If you don't want it, give it back."

"I'll have a sip," said the man. "Thank you. That's what you say, isn't it?"

"If you're not a prick."

The man laughed. "And are you?"

"Only rarely."

"Charming."

"Do they always leave you like this? In the dark?"

"I'm used to the dark."

"I'm afraid you have the advantage on me, then. I'm only used to the dark for sleeping."

"Then sleep and save your strength, Peter Corbin of Providence. This vessel is a warren of bilge rats; they'll come to nibble your flesh soon enough."

Peter did not mean to sleep, but the fear and cold drained him. Between one blink and the next, his thoughts smeared as abstract brushstrokes, and he fell into dreams.

The dreams were not those to which he'd grown accustomed: grasping nightmares of the shelling thunder and the howls of agony rendered inhuman from human throats. The visions which now stalked his subconscious had a disturbing beauty to them.

He floated weightless among billows of slow-swinging ocean waves, beneath a sky pockmarked with faded, dark stars. He breathed, and slipped beneath the water.

He descended on shimmering currents, past twisted gardens of corals and pulsing, luminescent creatures which seemed neither animal nor plant. He fell until his feet touched the vast, pale emptiness of the sandy, abyssal plain. Around him swirled a snow-fall of detritus from the sunlit world, like the ice storm which had enveloped his home when he was a small boy, crystallizing the city as if it had been dipped in glass.

Before him loomed the carcass of some leviathan creature, shattered on the sand like a sacrificial bull. The corpse was swarmed by priests in the form of ghost-white crabs and writhing Gordian knots of slime-bathed hagfish. At the edges of his vision, something moved in the shadows.

Beyond the crumbling altar, an iridescent wall rose to unimaginable heights. Patterns of shifting colours arrested him, oily greens and purples with the same noxious beauty of spilled gasoline on the deck of a battleship.

The wall rippled, and a dark, jagged crack opened in the face of it. A black, horizontal split, like the letter 'W' written in a child's crude script.

When Peter was a boy, his father had taken him to a museum in Massachusetts, a curious building of narrow halls packed with yellowed glass jars of stinking formaldehyde. Peter had looked upon that same, crooked 'W' shape couched in the dead, staring eyes of a face from the deep. A face never meant to be seen by the light of God.

Above him, the colossal eye shifted and the pupil dilated to capture the faint light. The vast, implacable gaze cast down upon him, and Peter found himself captured in it. He opened his mouth to scream, and breathed seawater.

Peter jolted awake on the heels of phantom sensations, certain he was drowning. He swallowed back the mucus which had pooled in his mouth and choked out a cough to clear his airways of the chill, bilge-scented air.

"We're submerged," said the man, as if commenting on the weather. "I heard them operate the diving piano."

"Wonderful."

"Perhaps we'll be so fortunate to spring a leak."

Peter trembled. "I'd rather we didn't."

"You fear death?"

"You don't?"

"What is death but an eternal dream?"

"Death occupies my waking hours. I'd prefer to keep it out of my dreams."

"But you don't dream of death, do you? You dream of ancient, star-spawned things beneath the sea."

Shock clenched its cool fingers around Peter's throat. He transmuted the strangled sound into a laugh. "What, are you Daniel now?"

"Daniel?"

"From the holy books. Telling kings of men what it is they dream."

"Is that what Daniel is? A teller of dreams?"

"I should imagine so."

"Then perhaps I am Daniel."

"If you want to be Daniel, tell me what I dream."

The man made a sound of contemplation. "You dream of the ocean, the black expanse of the sunless desert, the watery sky above you."

"We're in a submarine. A lucky guess."

"Other times you dream of the trenches. You draw with bare fingers in the sticky mud. Faces of those you have known. Of the wife who left you."

Blood drained from Peter's face. "How do you know that?"

"A lucky guess. Or I am Daniel. What are you, Peter Corbin?"

"I'm a soldier."

"That is what you do, not what you are."

"I was a painter. Before the Great War."

"What did you paint?"

"Landscapes," Peter lied.

"Truly?"

"What did you do? Before the war?"

"I wandered."

"A vagabond, you mean?"

"The details do not matter. I existed outside. Beyond the edge of a cosmos which pulsed with light and noise. And yet none of the light could touch me."

"That seems a lonely existence."

"Only rarely."

"And now you are here, in a den of darkness and lions?"

"An ignoble end."

"But that's not the whole story, is it?" Peter asked

"No?"

"The lions warmed Daniel, eased his loneliness in the king's prison. Even in the lion's den, there was hope."

"Is that so?"

"We keep cats in our beds. And what is a cat but a very small lion?"

The man laughed, and the sound warmed Peter's empty belly. "So it is. Drink your water, Peter. I can't say when or if they'll feed you."

Time passed in unknown quantities. The Germans did not feed them. Peter rationed the water in the canteen. Daniel did not ask for any.

A gunshot rang out in the dark. Beyond the bulkhead, he heard a scuffle, voices raised in strident German. He held still as a hedge rabbit as three more shots rang out, followed by silence.

"Daniel?"

"Don't be afraid," said Daniel. "Just rats, fighting amongst themselves."

Before he could respond, the bulkhead opened, and light sliced across his eyes. Under watery lids, he watched the familiar shadow of a soldier loom over him.

"So," said the soldier, "you are still alive."

"Yes."

"You said the name of the man. The one we pulled from the water."

"Lieutenant Radcliffe?"

"Who was he?"

"My commanding officer."

"No. Who was he, Ami?"

"I don't understand."

"Can you hear it?"

"What?"

"The voice in the shadows."

"I don't know what you're talking about."

The soldier watched him. The backlit halo of his helmeted head cast his features in deep shadow. "The Lieutenant says it is mutiny, but I say it is fever. A pestilent restlessness which poisons the mind."

"I don't understand what you're saying."

"I watched Klenze and Zimmer tear out each other's throats. They fell to violence, shrieking about voices in the dark. The Lieutenant put them down like rabid dogs. Schmidt was found dead in his bunk, unmarked, with his eyes wide open."

"I did nothing!"

"You brought something onto this vessel, dog. Something evil."

"Are you blaming me? I've been here, right where you left me. We both have."

"We?"

"The other American."

"Understand this, Ami," said the soldier. "You are the only living soul we brought aboard this vessel. I told them to cast it overboard, the clay monstrosity. It and you together. A burial at sea."

Peter said nothing.

"But it is too late for that, I think. This place is infected, a den of sickness. We were touched by pestilence the moment we pulled you from the water."

"What do you want from me? I don't believe there was anyone sick aboard the *Valor*."

"Believe what you want, Ami. The officers feel the same. But there is something down here with us."

The pitiless clang of the closing bulkhead echoed in Peter's bones.

"Who are you?" said Peter.

"You called me Daniel," said the voice in the dark.

"That's a lie."

"Is it?"

"You said you were an American soldier."

"You asked me if I was on the *Valor*."

"You were?"

"What do you think?"

"I don't know what to think." Hot tears pricked at the edges of Peter's eyes. "I lied," he said, as if to the confessional.

"Did you?"

"I didn't paint landscapes. I painted people."

"What sort of people?"

"Wealthy men and women for whom law and money were no object. Who wanted their private desires woven into tapestries of deniability and immortalized in oil. Bare as the denizens of Eden. Wrapped in one another and clothed only in ecstasy."

"Tell me."

"The first time, a man came to me with his wife. They wished to be portrayed as Eros and Psyche."

"And did you do it?"

"They undressed each other while I prepared my canvas. We draped the table in red."

"Was she beautiful?"

"The man asked me to draw them coupled."

"In front of you?"

"He must have seen my shock. 'So you can get her expression right', he said." Peter shivered. "He was correct, I confess. Her face was beatific, like a saint in religious ecstasy. It took an hour, maybe more. They barely moved the entire time, like marble statues."

"Did it stir you? To see her that way?"

"Sometimes he would touch her. He didn't have to look. He knew her by feel. Like a sculptor."

"Did you want her?"

"Her control was impeccable," Peter said, rather than answering. "As was his. When I finished, he removed himself from her, as stoic as if he were arranging himself for dinner."

He did not say how he had been unable to watch the man help his wife to dress, how the tender domesticity of their movements was too intimate and obscene for his gaze. He did not say how the man's eyes had held him, deep, unnerving, and full of insight. *I see you*, those eyes had said. *You are like me.*

"Regardless," Peter said, "the money was good."

"Only the money?"

"Others came. Women from Boston who desired to be portrayed as lovers of Sappho. Men entwined as Bacchus and his satyrs. Beautiful heretics who cavorted in the shadows. Their money allowed me to paint my nightmares."

"And what was in those nightmares?"

"Before the war? A kaleidoscope of hideous beauty. Now? Only the screams of the dying and the silence of the dead."

"Horrors too mundane for the cultured artist?"

"No," said Peter. "Exactly mundane enough."

"You should drink some water."

Peter spat a bit of phlegm into the darkness. "Why? I'm dead regardless."

"You should still drink."

"What does a creature of shadow care about the death of one nobody?"

"Is that what you think I am?"

"Was it a game? A lion playing with his prey?"

"Didn't the lions warm Daniel? Permit him to dry his tears in their yellow manes?"

"I don't know."

For the first time, Peter heard something move in the space near him. A strange, squelching sound. "You don't have to fear me, Peter."

"No?"

"I do regret that we encountered each other in such direct fashion. We might have met in passing. A pestilent yellow fog which crept along your door. A golden drop of kerosene to illuminate the last frenzied moments in which you painted a portrait that brought men to tears. The fleeting passage of a dark star in the skies of Providence, to bring you dreams of beautiful horrors and bleed them out under the edge of your pallet knife."

"There's nothing for me back in Providence."

"Nothing?"

"No family. And my wife was right to leave me."

"Do you miss her?"

"Often."

"Did you love her?"

Daniel shut his eyes against the words. "Yes, but not as the priests say a man should love his wife."

"I see."

"Do you?"

"I see a man moulded of grief, with sorrow fired into his bones. A man who offered a stranger a sip of water in the blackened pit."

"How could I do anything else?"

"You'd be surprised."

Something boneless and wet brushed Peter's face, and he flinched. It coiled beneath his eye, wiped at the tracks of his tears. In a moment of madness, he leaned into it, desperate for gentleness in the dark.

"There is a word," said Daniel, "in the language of the Greeks. A word for a man's finest moment, and sometimes his last. Achilles in the Trojan sunlight. Pygmalion in the battlefield of marble dust. The absolute realization of potential. The madness of creative fervour. A state of grace. Do you remember it, Peter?"

Peter shook, his face numb and tingling. "Yes."

"Do you know why you are here?"

"Because you brought me here?"

"Because that which is in you called to that in me."

"What are you?"

"I am what haunts the long dark of the soul. A fear and a shadow. I rule the madness of poets, of playwrights, of painters, of sculptors. My domain is the spark of creation to which you cleave. You are here, Peter, because you were always meant to be mine."

Flesh so slick it carried the illusion of softness passed over his skin. The sensation raised goosebumps on him, the fevered dreams of the lonely fisherman's wife.

Daniel unbuttoned his uniform with what felt like hundreds of grasping arms. "I can't warm you, or purr for you," he said. "But I would ease your loneliness, if you let me."

"Please."

"Have you ever been with a man?"

"Many times," said Peter.

"No matter," said Daniel. "It would have taught you nothing here."

A hand pressed itself against Peter, and he felt the prick of a knife at his throat. "Do you hear it?" said the soldier.

Peter remained still, uncertain if he was expected to answer.

"Do you fucking hear it?"

"The voice?"

"No, pig. Fucking listen."

"I don't hear anything."

"And why would that be?"

Peter's heart skipped a beat. "The engines."

"'The engines', he says. Yes, the fucking engines!"

Peter said nothing.

The soldier exhaled a fetid breath in his face. "They called me *Dachschaden,* did you know that? Müller the Mad One, always whining about demons and darkness with teeth. The Lieutenant believed in nothing but money and blood. But I've seen, Ami. I'm an old hare. I've seen the devils which stalk the trenches, not made for mortal minds or mortal eyes."

"What do you want from me?"

"Why are you still alive? Why haven't you bitten your tongue and drowned in the blood?"

"I don't know."

"Is it here, with us? Is He here?"

"I don't know."

"It likes you, doesn't it? If I slit your throat, would it stop the blood?"

Peter didn't dare reply.

Müller laughed, ugly and hysterical. "We've no way up, Ami. No way to chart our course or control our depth. We're drifting in the current. Too deep for light."

"I'm sorry."

"He wants me to put a bullet between my eyes, did you know that? Or slit my throat and baptize the steel like a bullock on an ancient Roman altar. Or pass willingly up through the hatch and into the jaws of watery death. He whispers to us. Words of madness. Words of sickness. One by one, they fell to it. A monster stalks these depths, Ami. And, God in Heaven, I should have cast you back into the Sargasso and taken my whipping like a martyr."

"Are you going to kill me?"

"I should. And yet I wonder if it's crueller to leave you to fall into the hands of that thing."

Peter squeezed his eyes shut in the darkness, and kept silent.

Müller spat something virulent which Peter didn't recognize, and the knife left his throat. He heard the man cross the metal floor. Heard the creak of the failing components, a fragile shell which barely held back the unfathomable abyss of the ocean around them.

"Wise men know," said Müller, "how one should only worship dead gods. Enjoy your tomb, Ami."

He left, a vacuum of fear and recycled air in his wake. Peter rolled onto his side and began to claw at his chained wrist.

"Please," he whispered. His skin split beneath ragged nails. "Please, please, please."

"Peter," said Daniel.

"No, no, no, you're not real. You're a delusion of fear and hunger." He twisted like an animal in a trap. Could he break the bones? Bite off the fingers?

"Peter."

"You're not real!"

"Peter, you're hurting yourself."

"Fuck you!"

"You're angry."

"I want to go home!" Tears spilled down his cheeks. "I want out. I don't want to die down here!"

"Peter."

Rage metastasized in his belly. "If you're real, why don't you help me? What is it you want?"

"I want you to stop tearing at your skin."

"Fuck off. If you're as powerful as he thinks, why are we trapped here?"

"It's not so simple. Is death really the worst you can imagine?"

"I don't care. I'll do anything to stay alive."

"Anything?"

"Yes. Why? Do you want my soul?" Peter laughed bitterly. "I've heard the priests. It was destined for Hell anyway."

"I'm certain your soul is quite beautiful, but no."

"Then what do you want?"

Something damp stroked Peter's hair, cool against skin flushed hot by angry tears.

Daniel sighed, the sound jarring in its humanity. "Very well," he said. "I accept your offer."

"My offer of what?"

Powerful coils rippled up around his limbs like binding serpents. "Try to relax," said Daniel.

Peter clutched at Daniel with his unbound hand, offering a pathetic resistance as his fingers slid among now-familiar tendrils. "I don't understand."

Appendages which had brought comfort and ecstasy now turned cruel and implacable. The ringed teeth of the suckers which lined them pricked the skin of Peter's face. His head was encased in vermiculate coils.

"Daniel?"

"Try to be still."

Around them, the metal of the submarine groaned like a dying beast. In the depths of the vessel, Peter heard Müller scream.

Daniel cradled his face tenderly, and Peter's heart broke.

"I'm truly sorry, Peter," said Daniel, and then unspeakable agony pierced his eyes.

It was a nurse named Dorothy who changed Peter's bandages. An army surgeon had removed the gelatinous ruins of his eyes and packed the sockets with gauze. He'd run a fever, they told him. A frightful delirium in which he'd sobbed and begged for help, for mercy, and for a man named Daniel.

He'd been picked up by a fishing vessel in Narragansett Bay, waterlogged, dehydrated, and hundreds of miles from where the *Valor* had sunk. He had no memory of the event. He'd been clothed in a life vest and wrapped in a shroud of sargassum. The fishermen had identified him by the dog tags at his throat and submitted his unconscious body to the naval hospital in Newport, where, for lack of family, he remained.

"What did you do?" said Dorothy. "Before the war, I mean."

"I painted," he said.

"I suppose you'll not be doing so much of that anymore."

"No," he said. "I suppose not."

Yet it was Dorothy who brought him a lump of sculptor's clay, firm and malleable between his fingers. Bereft of anything to do but heal, he wrought it into the patterns of his private nightmares.

"What is that?" she asked him one day. "An octopus?"

"A shadow of one," he told her.

"Still," she said, "rather fascinating."

Her words followed him through the mundane misery to procure his soldier's pension and the domestic dance to find a house girl to help him navigate his home on Benefit Street. He settled at last on a young woman named Genevieve, with a gentle voice and cold hands, who filled the house with the scent of baked bread and lured neighbourhood cats to the garden with dishes of cream.

Thus ensconced, Peter rose and slept. Sculpted and sat in the warm glow of the sleeping porch, encased in the tangible remembrance of sunlight. Shaped the horrors of his dreams in clay. He procured a slate and stylus and began to learn the patterns of Braille which would let him write again. Sometimes Genevieve would sit and read to him. Sometimes he would sleep and fall into nightmares of the ocean depths. Sometimes he wondered if the nightmare had ever been real.

It was August, and the summer air was pea soup. He woke, disgruntled and exhausted, to a tap on his bedroom door.

"Mr Corbin?" said Genevieve. "You've got a visitor."

"A visitor? Surely not."

"Says he's a friend. Smart suit on him."

"I don't have any friends left alive. Did he give a name?"

"Mr Thurston."

Peter rolled out of bed to seek his slippers and cane. *Look at you*, he thought. *Barely forty and you're an old man.*

"Shall I put him in the living room?"

"Yes, thank you, Genevieve."

It was Genevieve who'd thought to sew an extra button on the inside of the hem of his shirts, marked in different locations so he could identify them. Peter would have just as soon worn the same shirt. He made himself presentable and began the slow descent from the second floor to the foyer.

As he reached the bottom of the stairs he heard the clink of china. "Here you are, Mr Thurston."

"Thank you, my dear," said Daniel's voice.

Peter swayed and caught himself on the wall.

"Mr Corbin?" said Genevieve.

Peter gripped the crook of his cane and found his voice. "Yes, Genevieve, give me a moment." He braced himself on cane and plaster, took a few unsteady steps into the living room. "Would you give us some privacy?"

"Of course, Mr Corbin."

He listened to her leave. "Thurston, is it?"

"If you like. But you know my name."

"Do I?"

"You know the name by which you loved me, and that is just as good."

"Did I?"

For the first time since they'd met in the pit of darkness, Daniel's tone took on a hint of uncertainty. "You tell me."

"Give me your hand."

He heard Daniel rise from the couch, the squeak of a floorboard as he passed over it. A hand took his own: human fingers and human warmth.

Peter gripped at the woollen fabric of Daniel's sleeves. "I don't understand."

"A pretence, like the name. A corpse-cloak of humanity stitched over a shadow."

"I take it there's a body missing from the morgue?"

"It's only a tool."

"My God."

"Not that one."

Peter pressed his palm to his lips and could not answer.

"But," said Daniel, "a tool I hoped to use for you. To sit beside you in the sunlight."

"Are you asking me if I would keep a small lion in my bed?"

"In a manner of speaking."

A watery laugh escaped Peter's lips. "Then will you kiss me?"

"Of course."

The gesture was as soft as the touch of a butterfly's wings. A warm and golden breath of sunshine, ripe with the promise of new ideas and new beginnings.

"Come," Peter said, when they parted. "Let me show you my sculptures."

THE MIDNIGHT DIYU

Melissa Ren

Melissa Ren *is a Chinese-Canadian writer whose narratives tend to explore the intersection between belonging and becoming. She is a prize recipient of* Room Magazine's *Fiction Contest, a Tin House alum, a grant recipient of the Canada Council for the Arts, and a senior editor at Augur Magazine. Her writing has appeared or is forthcoming in* Grain Magazine, Factor Four Magazine, Fusion Fragment, *and elsewhere. Find her at linktr.ee/MelissaRen or follow her on various socials* @melisfluous.

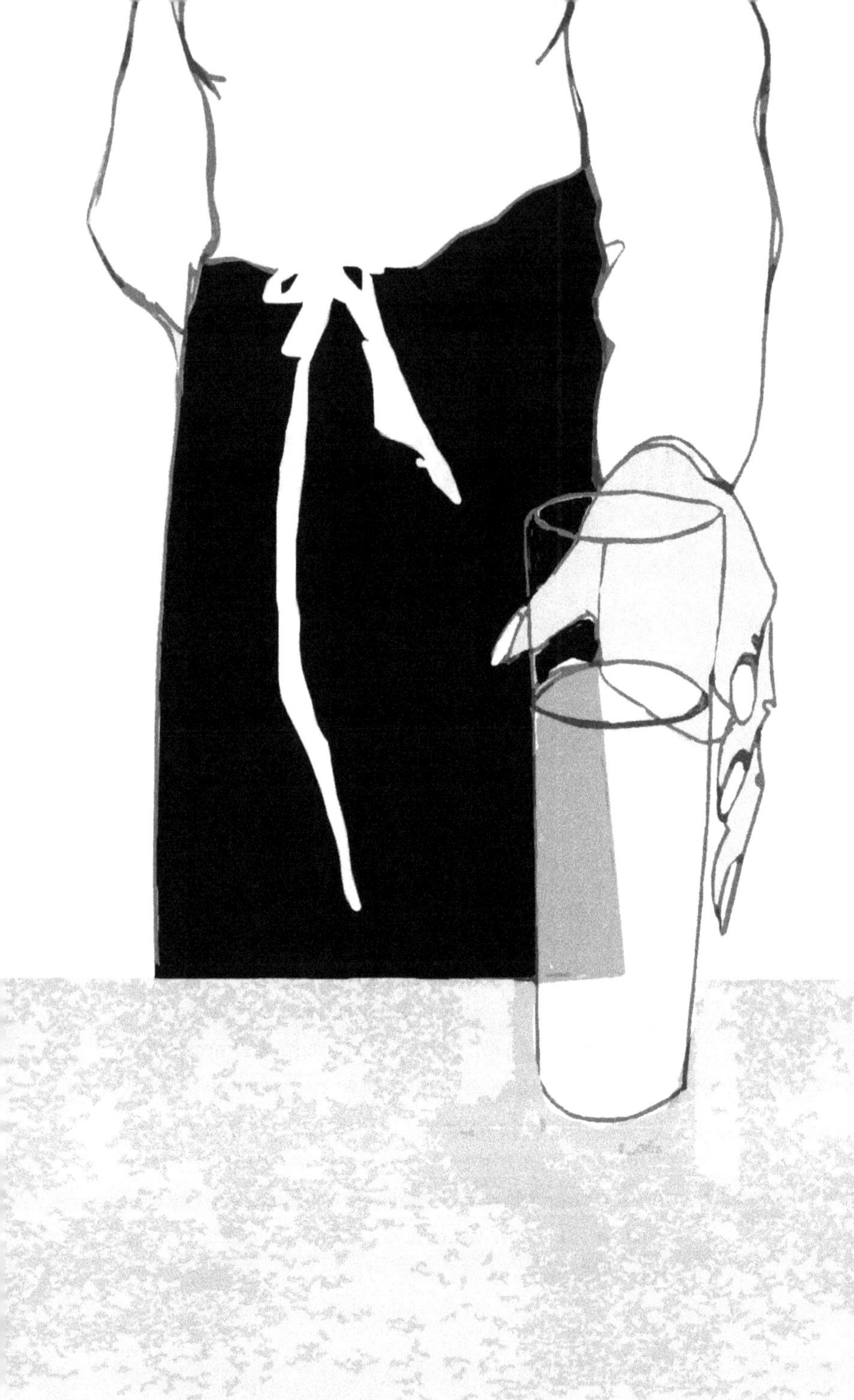

$\mathscr{T}$HE MIDNIGHT DIYU

The bell chimed as the front door swung open. My head snapped up from my crossword.

A man walked in. He was about my age, with a striking face and killer jawline. Fuck, what a shame. He wore a bomber jacket, jeans with a distressed knee, and black Chucks. He bore no visible wounds or bruises. Carbon monoxide, maybe?

As expected, he stood by the entrance and glanced at the globed red lantern lurking overhead. Its red tassels fluttered in response to the oscillating fan mounted at the corner of the wall.

"Sit anywhere you like," I said.

The man ambled forward and parked his ass in front of me at the counter. I raised a brow; no one ever did that. People usually scurried into the corner or sat by the window to gaze out at the darkness. Instead, he had gravitated towards me, the only warm body, though I was always cold.

Up close, he had a creamy complexion with the most luscious skin I'd ever seen, like he cleansed his face with oat milk. I bet his skin was soft, too. What a waste.

He leaned forward, his eyes roaming behind me as if searching for something in particular. I poured him a glass of water. He was likely parched; they usually were.

I tipped my chin at him. "What can I get you?"

He chugged the drink in a single swig, then gasped as he set down the glass and swiped the back of his hand over his mouth. "Can I get another?" His voice was deep and scratchy, as if dragged over gravel.

After I topped him up, he took measured sips, then met my eyes. Two obsidian coins, glossy, almost. My stomach warmed.

"Hungry?" I asked.

"Famished."

I tilted my head, assessing his taste buds. "Something greasy?"

"Definitely."

Bet he liked seafood. "Salt and pepper deep fried squid?"

"That's my favourite."

Mine too. "I had a feeling." Why the hell was I smiling? Was I flirting? What the hell was wrong with me?

I put through the order and returned to refill his glass.

"What time is it?" He raked a hand through his hair. This was the point when shit could get awkward.

I checked my watch. "Three in the morning."

"You always work the night shift?"

I nearly smiled again. The dead usually freaked out, wondering where the fuck they were. Some threw up. Some cried. Others inspected their wounds. But most had questions I couldn't answer. Once, a guy banged his head against the wall, hoping he'd wake up from this nightmare. No such luck. This was a one-way ticket to hell. And once I filled their bellies, they went on their merry way. The Midnight Diyu was just a pit stop, like its namesake, Diyu — a purgatory for the unliving.

But this guy was calm and chatty, an unlikely combo for someone in his state.

Maybe he didn't know what had happened to him. Perhaps he'd died in his sleep and 'woken up' here. Though that didn't explain why he was dressed like he'd been out kicking it with his boys.

God, I hated playing messenger to the dead. Best to ease him into his new reality. "The night shift's quieter, but there are rushes now and then."

"The after-club crowd, huh?" Yeah, he had no fucking clue.

"Is that where you were?" It would explain the outfit. And his model hair. Maybe he'd ODed?

"God, no," he said with a laugh. "I was actually on my way to work." So, he worked the night shift, too.

"And you decided to take a detour to grab some food instead?" Did he jump off a bridge? I eyed him sceptically. That would've roughed him up for sure, and his skin was perfectly intact. "Very responsible of you."

He smiled, completely oblivious of his demise. "Like I said, I was heading to work."

"You work in the food service industry, too?"

Instead of answering me, he scoped out the area behind me before whipping around as if responding to a name call. His elbow sent his glass flying. Water gushed to the floor. "Shit." He jumped to his feet.

I snatched the mop and cleaned up the mess. "Don't worry about it." I rested the handle against the counter.

He brushed off his pants. His gaze raked down my body. My insides liquefied. He shook his head and muttered, "A damn pity."

My brows snapped together. What the hell did that mean?

The man shrugged off his jacket and tossed it on the counter as he rounded it. He filled a glass with water.

"Hey, you can't go back there. It's for employees only."

"You thirsty?" He set a glass of water on the counter. "You look thirsty."

My throat suddenly burned, like a match scraping its strip. Without thinking, I gulped the water. Cool relief swam down my throat, coating it like honey. As soon as I finished, a fire rushed up my oesophagus.

"More," I croaked, tapping the glass.

He smiled and crooked a brow.

The entrance door flung open. A gust ripped the bell off its hinges, and it sputtered across the floor. Wind tumbled along the beige tile and travelled up my body. Goosebumps sprouted from my skin.

The empty door frame glowed with a crimson halo that pulsed like a heartbeat. A chill skittered over my skin, and the wind whistled *my* name.

They only summoned the dead.

"No," I breathed. I clasped my chest and yanked my hand back at the dampness. Blood stained my palm.

No.

"I gotta clock in." The man wrapped an apron around his waist and nudged his chin towards the door. "Looks like your shift is over."

I CAN'T TELL YOU THAT

William Kitcher

William Kitcher's stories, plays, and comedy sketches have been published, produced, and/or broadcast in Australia, Belgium, Bosnia and Herzegovina, Canada, Czechia, England, Germany, Guernsey, Holland, India, Ireland, Nigeria, Singapore, South Africa, Sweden, the US, and Wales. His comic noir novel, Farewell And Goodbye, My Maltese Sleep, was published in October 2023 by Close To The Bone Publishing, and is available on Amazon.

I Can't Tell You That

Of course I was suspicious. A guy gives you a grand and tells you to go to a bar out in the sticks. I was suspicious of anything Darrell said, especially when I didn't know if he knew I'd screwed him around on the last job. So I went to some town that could have been in one of the Dakotas but was actually in Ontario. Somewhere between Nowhere and Armpit.

The main drag was short. On one side of the street, separated by empty lots, were a grocery store, a pharmacy, a bar, and a gas station that was closed and looked like it had been closed for twenty years. Behind the stores were an abandoned railroad track and a vague attempt at a forest. The other side of the street had half a dozen houses, none of which had lights on.

I parked in front of the bar and made sure I locked all the doors.

I went inside, and the only humans there were a bartender and one guy sitting at the bar, drinking beer. Next to an old cash register, that had probably been there since the bar originally opened, sat two cats. They turned briefly to me and then went back to being cats.

At the back of the bar were a pool table and a dartboard. It seemed to me to be kind of dangerous to have them near each other, especially with alcohol involved. I sat, ordered a scotch, and waited.

Some guy came in. I didn't like the look of him, but then again I don't like the look of most people. "Garrett?" he asked. He was still standing there so I looked at him. "Are you Garrett?"

I shook my head.

The guy went to the bar and sat beside the other guy. "Are you Garrett?"

"Yeah," said the guy, and that surprised me because I'm Garrett.

The two of them talked for a while, then left. I went to the door and watched them. They walked until they got to the gas station, then stopped and talked. Then the newer guy took a knife out of his jacket and stabbed the first guy. He dragged the body into the woods behind the gas station. When the guy appeared on the street again, I popped back inside.

The guy came in, talked quietly to the bartender, and then left. The bartender picked up a phone and called someone. I couldn't hear what he said.

After a while, two cop cars and an ambulance drove past and stopped in front of the gas station. There were no sirens or flashing red lights; I guess it wasn't that important.

Some other guy came into the bar. It sure was a busy place for a one- or two-horse town. He was a slightly seedy forty, with an advancing forehead. If he'd been wearing a trench coat, he would have looked a bit like Dick Tracy from the old comics. He said to me, "You're Garrett."

I said nothing.

"I know you are," he said. "I'm Victor. I'm a friend of Darrell's."

"How do I know that?"

He described Darrell.

"That doesn't mean anything," I said. "You could've seen him somewhere. What's the name of his kid?"

"How the hell would I know that? Besides, I don't think he has a kid. I don't think Vera can have kids. Or maybe Darrell can't."

"OK."

"Darrell sent me after you. Thought you might need help."

"I don't even know what's going on."

A uniformed cop came in and talked to the bartender. The cop turned, looked at me, and then came over. "So why did you stab that guy?"

"I didn't stab the guy. The bartender could have told you that. He could describe both guys."

"No, he couldn't," said the cop.

"I suppose you're right," I said.

Victor stepped forward. "Officer, I can vouch for this guy. He was in here the whole time."

"Who the hell are you?" said the cop.

Victor reached into the inside pocket of his jacket, pulled out a police badge, and flashed it. I suppose he looked like Dick Tracy for a reason.

The uniformed cop nodded his head, then left me there with Victor Tracy. Victor said, "That was weird. I would have assumed that any guy after you knows what you look like."

"But he didn't," I said. "He thought the other guy was me. Who was he?"

"No idea."

"What the hell is going on?"

"No idea. Darrell just told me to keep an eye on you."

"But you're a cop. Darrell's not exactly a friend of cops."

"You know how it is ..." He trailed off.

I knew how it was. "Uh-huh," I said.

"Besides, I'm off duty."

"What do we do now?"

"Dunno. Wanna play some pool?"

We played some pool. He wasn't a good enough player for me to be able to hustle a few bucks off him.

The cop cars and ambulance went by again the other way, not quickly. The uniformed cop who'd come in before re-entered and said to Victor, "The guy's dead."

"Who was he?"

"A guy from Toronto. John Winston."

"Yeah, no idea. Thanks," said Victor, chalking his cue.

The cop left.

I watched Victor miss another shot. I said, "That can't be a coincidence. Winston."

"It's not. That was Darrell's brother."

"Why the hell would Darrell's brother say he was me?"

"They don't get along. I guess he wanted to find out what was going on."

"He got killed! And the killer thought he killed me. Why would someone want to kill me?"

"Look at the bright side. Now he thinks you're dead."

I went outside and walked down to the gas station. There were no cops there, no crime scene, none of those yellow 'Do Not Cross' plastic strips tied around trees. *Right*, I thought, *the victim was from Toronto.* No big deal.

I went back to the bar and played some more pool with Victor.

Two women came into the bar. Jeesh, it was like Union Station in here. They went over to the bar, exchanged some words with the bartender, then came over to us, carrying a couple of shots of tequila, lime and all. One of them asked us if we wanted to play pool against them. We had nothing to do so we did.

We introduced ourselves. Neither Victor nor I gave our actual names. I was Bill and Victor was Danny. The short blonde was Allie; the taller brown-haired woman was Eddie. I didn't ask what that was short for. They probably weren't their real names anyway.

After the first game, Allie said to me, "You wanna go out back?"

I've never declined an offer like that from a hot blonde. Most of the time it didn't work out. Once, I got rolled.

Allie and I went out back. It was a dump, not much light, weeds everywhere, damaged concrete, construction site refuse, and other assorted junk. Garbage bags were being ripped apart by raccoons. They ignored us and continued their work. There was a beat-up truck about fifteen years old, but it was an F-150, so it probably still ran.

Allie said to me, "You're Garrett, right?"

I took a couple of steps away from her. "You're not gonna stab me, are you?"

She laughed. "I just have to get some shit. Darrell said you're good protection."

"What kind of shit do you have to get?"

"I can't tell you that."

"Can't Eddie help you?"

"She's tough, but not tough enough. Besides, she's a bank teller. Not a lot of use to me in a situation like this."

"What about, uh, Danny?"

"I don't know him."

"You don't know me."

"Darrell recommended you."

"Darrell recommended him."

"I don't know that."

"Neither do I," I said, knowing I would never understand this circular argument, let alone win it.

The beat-up F-150 was Allie's. We got into it, drove a couple of streets away, and pulled into a house's driveway. She got out of the truck, and I trailed behind. She didn't ring the bell or knock, just turned the doorknob. Nothing happened. With a well-placed kick of her boot, she kicked the door in.

No one was inside. Half-finished bottles of beer, full ashtrays, empty pizza boxes, the TV still on.

"They hurried out of here," said Allie. "I think I know where they went. You ready?"

"For what? I have no idea what's going on!"

"That's the way I want it."

We drove out into the backwoods, along a road that even a pack of hyenas would avoid. She turned off the truck lights, shut off the engine, and we cruised down a hill then pulled off to the side of the road. The moonlight showed three wrecked cars. They'd been there since last winter, she said, the result of some robbery that had gone really wrong. I didn't know why she was telling me this.

She took two flashlights out of the glove compartment, gave me one, and told me not to turn it on until she said so. She reached behind her, grabbed a baseball bat, and handed it to me.

"That's it? A bat?" I asked.

"They don't have guns. We're Canadian, remember?"

She put on an oversized bomber jacket, and we walked down the road for a minute or so then turned onto a driveway that was more an overgrown path. I tripped. "Walk carefully," she said, pointlessly.

There was a shack, and no one was in it.

"I know where they are," she said. "There are caves out back. Bootleggers used to use them. Now the local scumbags use them to stash stuff."

We staggered into the woods. Well, I did. Allie seemed to know where she was walking.

"See that stand of birch?" she whispered. "The cave entrance is right behind that. When we get there, I'll give you a signal. Turn on your flashlight and just wave it around into the cave. I'll do the same, and it'll seem like there are a lot of us. Then I want you to tell them we're the cops, and that if they throw the shit out, nothing will happen to them. They'll believe you. They won't recognize your voice, and, well, the cops around here …" She trailed off, and I understood what she meant and believed her.

We got to the cave, she gave me the signal, I waved my flashlight around, so did she. She took out her phone and aimed a flashing red light into the cave. Kinda looked like a lame movie premiere. I dropped my voice into a lower register, told them we were the cops. Whoever was in the cave yelled a few obscenities. Allie put her phone away, took a gun out of her jacket, and fired a few shots in the direction of the cave, deliberately not into it.

A cardboard box came flying out. Allie picked it up, glanced inside, then looked at me and nodded. We ran like hell, she being more hell than me as she was way ahead.

By the time I'd found the driveway and made it back to the road, Allie was waiting for me with the truck running. I got in, and she floored it.

We drove back to town, Allie parked the truck in the same space behind the bar, and we went inside. That seemed weird. Why didn't she just run?

Eddie and Victor were still playing pool.

"Mission accomplished," said Allie.

I had no idea what was going to happen next, so we played some more pool. I kept looking at the bartender, but he ignored me.

Five guys came into the bar. I could guess who they were. One of them was the guy who'd stabbed Darrell's brother. They focused on Allie, and moved towards her. She picked up the cue ball and whipped it right into Stabber's face. This seemed to be the right thing to do. I picked up a couple of balls and threw but missed. Eddie took the darts out of the dartboard and launched them. The cats disappeared under the bar. So did Victor. Allie picked up a pool cue and whomped one of them right in the kisser. That was enough for the boys, and they split.

The bartender laughed as he picked up the stray balls and darts.

We drank more. I didn't know what else to do.

At the end of the night, the bar closed, the bartender kicked us out, and we went out back. Allie's truck windows had been smashed, and there were a few pointless divots on the hood. She searched the truck but didn't find the box. She said, "Crap." Allie and Eddie got into the truck and were gone really quickly.

Victor said to me, "You know they were cops, right?"

"No," I said, defeated.

"Yeah. Cops around here. You know …"

"Yeah, I guess I do. Why did I have to go with Allie if Eddie is a cop?"

"I guess she had to keep an eye on me." Victor kicked a half-eaten apple towards the raccoons. "You could have made a little bonus if it had worked out. Darrell said something about ten grand. But I guess you end up with only a grand because Darrell knows you screwed him around on your last job. But maybe you'll get a bonus because his brother is dead."

I leaned up against the wall of the bar. "Your name's not Victor, is it?"

"No."

"What is it?"

"I can't tell you that."

"Are you actually a cop?"

"I can't tell you that. Do you need a ride back to Toronto?"

"Nah, I have a car." And there was no way I was going back to Toronto. Darrell knew my last address. Maybe I'd go on to Montreal.

Victor left. I went around to the front of the bar and got into my car. The bartender came out and knocked on my window. I rolled it down and he passed me a bulging envelope.

I looked in it and must have seemed surprised because the bartender laughed. "Darrell was apparently going to give you ten, so we're giving you more. You were going to make out whichever way things went down. Pretty shrewd, man. But you made the right choice."

Shrewd? Hell, yes. I thought I was still working for Darrell.

And then something occurred to me. "Why would Allie come back to the bar after she'd gotten the box of whatever it was? Why didn't she just take off with it?"

"When she first came in, I told her Darrell said for her to wait here until further notice …"

"Nicely done. And why did those guys bother to come inside the bar after they'd stolen the box?"

"They think they're tougher than cops. They're not that bright."

I laughed. I put my hand out the window and he shook it. "I'm Brooks," I said. "What's your name?"

"I can't tell you that."

No one tells you much these days. Maybe it's better not to know. I'll have to learn how to say 'I can't tell you that' in French.

M4R1NA

Mike Carson

Mike Carson *is a living testament to the truth of Douglas Adams's observation, "It takes an awful lot of time to not write a book." In his years of literary procrastination and steady weight gain, however, Mike has managed to publish several short stories and essays, win a few writing awards, and survive thirty-five years as a high school teacher. He lives in Kamloops with his wife and family, still teaching and working away at not writing a book. This story won the 2024 Jack Whyte Storyteller's Award at the Surrey International Writers' Conference. Previous SiWC contest honourable mentions of Mike's have appeared in* Pulp Literature *issues 26, 38, and 46.*

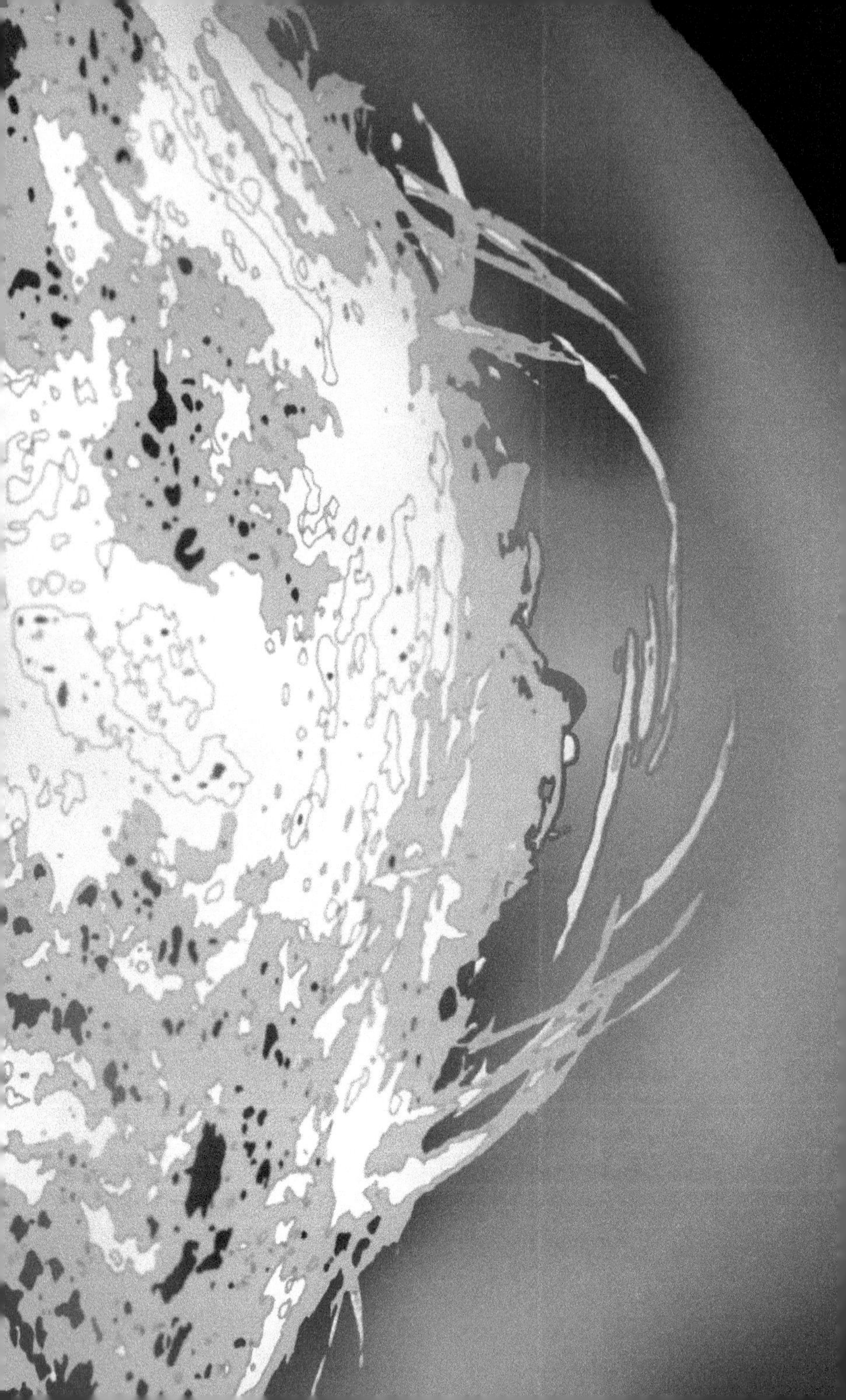

M4RINR

It begins with the eruption of a solar flare. Eight point three minutes later, a burst of electromagnetic radiation washes over the Earth's atmosphere, the resulting geomagnetic storm temporarily disrupting satellite communications, GPS systems, and causing isolated power outages in remote regions of the northern hemisphere. Hunched at his desk at NASA's Solar Dynamics Observatory, Dr Martin Welliver watches his monitors fade to black as the force of the X-class flare overloads one pyranometer after another. "Beautiful," he says. "Like the breath of God."

Had God—or anyone else—been around to hear him, it is unlikely they would have cared. Aside from some minor inconveniences—and an unprecedented display of aurora borealis lighting up the night skies from Fort Lauderdale to Fairbanks for several days following—the solar flare has little effect on the lives of Earth's 8.7 billion inhabitants. It is on another world, nearly 800 million miles away, that something extraordinary happens.

It takes the solar flare another 73 minutes to reach Saturn, where it dances across the E ring before streaking away again into the void, ionized particles of ancient dust and ice trailing behind it like the outstretched wings of some iridescent bird as it soars across the ice-locked surface of the tiny moon, Enceladus. There, the touch of the solar flare imbues a spark of life. In an icy fissure, where the temperature holds steady at two hundred degrees below zero, a small, red light begins to glow as M4RINR, Thoth Corporation's state-of-the-art-rover-turned-five-billion-dollar-failure, comes alive at last.

Piggybacking on NASA's interstellar probe, *Wanderer 2*, it took five years for M4RINR (affectionately dubbed '*Mariner*') to reach Enceladus. Its orbit was perfect. Its descent was perfect. Its landing, perfect. The engineers and scientists at Thoth Corp congratulated one another profusely, then returned to their monitors, certain that soon M4RINR would begin transmitting evidence that some form of life existed in the liquid plumes or subterranean oceans of Enceladus. But no signal ever came. For two years, M4RINR remained silent. After much finger-pointing, a few rounds of layoffs, media cover-ups, and the very public firing of M4RINR team lead and chief scapegoat Zoriana Boyko, the little rover was mostly forgotten. M4RINR remained where it had landed, a strange, dark blotch on a frozen, alien landscape, as the ice entombed it.

Silent, until today.

On another, more familiar, planet 746 million miles away, Sam McCarty leans heavily on his cane, watching the last mallard drake skitter across the ice-rimmed pond, a feathered frenzy of flapping and honking rising up to join the trailing end of the rapidly vanishing formation. "Godspeed," Sam says when the long, outstretched V has faded from sight. Some trick of topography and acoustics carries one final haunting cry to his ears. It sounds like farewell. He turns and begins limping up the rocky path, keenly aware of a dull ache deep in his chest.

Sam pauses at the top of the hill, breathing in the cool autumn air, the faintest tang of wood smoke on the breeze. The familiar ruin of the overgrown cabin squats before him, nearly hidden behind a jumble of radio antennae and satellite dishes, its peeling paint and crumbling chimney testament to Sam's losing battle with entropy. Huck lies on the porch, legs twitching. As Sam nears, the German shepherd lifts his head, drumming his tail against the peeling plywood decking. That is all. There was a time when the dog ran with the fleetness and wild abandon of his wolfish ancestors, and all the lesser creatures of forest and field fled before him. Now, the dog's days are spent asleep in the leaf-dappled sunshine, dreaming of younger days, dreams stretching slowly towards oblivion. Soon, Sam knows, the porch will be empty. At the top of the stairs, he stoops to pet the grizzled head of the last dog he will ever own.

Inside, Sam lights the stove and puts the kettle on the burner ring. A tidy array of ham radio equipment faces the bay window at the front of the small cabin. The rest of the interior is crowded with books: books on sagging shelves, books piled on the floor and the arms of the musty sofa. He picks up a tattered volume of Keats' poetry and thumbs through its worn pages. "'Half in love with easeful Death', indeed," Sam says, tossing the book aside. All its old magic has faded. "Sixty spins around the sun," he says. "Maybe that's enough; thirty-five more than Keats had."

Mug in hand, Sam shuffles towards the radio set, pausing out of habit before the portrait hanging on the wall between the kitchen and the front room. He hardly recognizes the version of himself smiling down from behind the fly-specked glass. In the photograph, his daughter, Charlotte—Charlie—dressed in a frilly fairy costume, holds a magic wand aloft. "Abracadabra, Mommy," she is saying. "Now you're a princess." It is her tenth birthday, when magic is real, when any obstacle can be overcome with the right incantation. Beside her, Sam's wife, Jana, presses her hands to the sides of her face in mock surprise. Everyone is happy. Sam searches the picture for some premonitory shadow that might have foretold the doom hanging over them all, but the sky is blue and clear and will be forever inside that dusty frame.

Six years from the day that photograph was taken, Charlie was gone, poisoned by false friends and anonymous strangers spewing dark things into cyberspace, toxic words and images that slithered into his daughter's mind through screens and earbuds to steal her self-worth, her innocence, her future. It is impossible for Sam to reconcile the child in the photograph with the pale, lifeless husk they found in Charlie's room that bleak October morning.

He and Jana limped on together for a few years after Charlie's death, but there was a frozen void between them that could never be crossed or filled. Their parting was amicable in the way that two icebergs drifting apart is amicable. They sold the house, and Jana headed to Vancouver to lose herself in the crowd. Sam moved to the cabin with his dog, his books, and his radio, trying to lose himself in words and the distant sounds of the universe. He knew better than anyone that there was nothing worth listening to on Earth.

Sam sinks into the office chair, sets down his tea, and powers up the system, hearing the familiar pop and crackle of the speakers. Once, he had listened with what was almost hope to signals from the farthest reaches of the galaxy. Long into the night, he would hunch over the control board, intent, fine-tuning dials, shoulders tense, straining to decipher a recognizable pattern from chaos, some staccato message from a distant world where, perhaps, another lonely creature was searching, too. He talked with astronauts on the ISS, picked up signals from the Deep Space Network and cryptic transmissions from military satellites, even heard the strange symphonies of the planets themselves. But in the turmoil of waves and frequencies resonating across the universe, Sam has yet to hear a message for him alone.

M4RINR's sensors come online first. It activates its onboard heating systems and ice drill and begins to burrow blindly in the direction its gyroscopic instruments indicate is up. M4RINR's ascent is slow. It must pause and heat the ice, then activate its drill before inching forward. Heat, drill, crawl, repeat. But all this effort requires energy, and M4RINR's is running dangerously low. Though equipped with a nuclear-fuelled thermoelectric generator capable of powering a small city for decades, a faulty relay buried somewhere in the miles-long labyrinth of wires, junctions, switches, and cables that form M4RINR's central nervous system makes it all but useless. The radioactive decay from the plutonium dioxide will keep M4RINR from freezing, but the rover will never be able to draw energy directly from the generator. M4RINR's motors begin slowing down, gears grinding. A barrage of failure alerts threatens to overload its CPU. The rover shuts down all unnecessary systems and pushes on through the crushing ice and unimaginable cold.

Finally, its drill pierces the outer crust, and the rover emerges onto the shimmering surface of Enceladus. M4R1NR deploys its solar panel array, but with more than half of the cells frozen solid, recharging the batteries will take much longer. Once sufficient power has been restored, M4R1NR extends its UHF antenna. Unable to establish a connection with the Deep Space Network, M4R1NR switches to a seldom-used frequency and transmits a distress call using lines of code from its Autonomous Research Gathering Operations System: ARGOS.

It takes ninety-three minutes for M4R1NR's message to cross the galaxy, streaking past planets and moons and DSN satellites, undetected by the vast telecom arrays of Thoth Corp and NASA and all the high-tech systems of Earth's superpowers. That whispered cry from out of the void might well have continued forever, unheard by human — or any other — ears, were it not for some cosmic design or quirk of physics that guided it far down into a lonely valley in northern British Columbia, where an old man sits at a ham radio, tuned in to the heavens, searching for some sign that the universe might not be as cold and empty as it seems.

Tonight, Sam focuses on a region of the solar system near Saturn. For several hours he scans and listens, scans and listens. He is about to quit for the night when he detects a high-pitched, repeating transmission too regular to be naturally occurring. His skin prickles. Leaning closer to the console, he adjusts the signal. It is unmistakable now. He reaches for a pen and a pad of paper and writes:

.- .-.. --- -. . / .- .-.. --- -. . / .- .-.. .-.. / .- .-.. .-.. / .- .-.. --- -. .

Morse code. Any radio operator worth a damn would recognize it. When he is finished translating, he leans back in his chair, stunned. "Alone alone all all alone" — words he has read a hundred times or more. Sam knows the stanza from Coleridge's *Rime of the Ancient Mariner* by heart:

Alone, alone, all, all alone,
Alone on a wide wide sea!
And never a saint took pity on
My soul in agony.

"Impossible," Sam says. *The Ancient Mariner* was one of Charlie's favourites. Night after night she would beg Sam to read it to her from *The Big Book of Illustrated Classics for Children*. She loved the almost Seussian rhyme of the poem and the wild, haunting images that accompanied the text. Charlie's favourite was the picture of the Polar Spirit who lived alone in the land of mist and snow. "The sea monster loved the bird, Daddy," she would say. "Why did the mariner kill the albatross?" Her eyes would brim with tears, tiny fingers tracing over the smudged image of the lonely sea creature. "Now he's all alone."

"I know, Charlie," Sam would say. "People can be cruel."

Sam knows he should notify someone, NASA perhaps. Instead, he rolls up to the keyboard and types his radio call sign, VA7PAJ, followed by the text, "Alone on a wide wide sea. Who are you?" The computer automatically broadcasts the message in Morse code; like tossing a bottle into the sea, those sine waves of sound might drift forever and never reach an inhabited shore. Sam leans back. He has no way of knowing how long the original signal had been travelling before it reached him, no way of knowing how long it will take for his message to travel back across the ocean of space even if, by some miracle, there is someone out there to hear it. Still, Sam can't help but smile in wonder at the strangeness of this sign, that has come to him out of the darkness like a tempest-tossed raven to raise the spectre of a hope he thought long dead.

Perhaps sensing some change in his master, Huck undertakes the Herculean task of tottering over to Sam's chair and dropping his head on his lap. Sam scratches the old dog between the ears. "Maybe there are more things in Heaven and Earth, old friend," Sam says.

M4R1NR's sensors begin documenting its surroundings: gravity, 0.0116 g; temperature, minus 235 degrees Celsius; atmospheric composition, 91 percent water, 4 percent nitrogen, 3.2 percent carbon dioxide, 1.7 percent methane. Geysers are erupting all around the little rover, massive fumaroles spewing water skyward. Much of the spray freezes instantly and rains back down in glittering droplets. With its forward cameras partially obscured by the crystalline blizzard, M4R1NR begins inching forward, its caterpillar tracks biting into the icy surface.

As it progresses through the maelstrom, M4R1NR receives a faint UHF message. Before it can respond, it detects a sudden spike in surface temperature. Without further warning, the crust of ice beneath the rover shatters. Since the surface gravity on Enceladus is approximately 1 percent of Earth's, M4R1NR's fall is more of a slow tumble, and the rover has been designed to take a beating. Unfortunately, its solar panels have not. Each time the rover bounces off one of the cavern walls or strikes an outcropping, more of the delicate arrays are destroyed.

M4RINR's calamitous twenty-kilometre descent to the bottom of the crevasse takes fourteen minutes. The damage it receives is neither catastrophic nor insignificant. Diagnostics reveal only minor structural damage and two broken cameras. The biggest issue is power: even a functioning array of solar panels would be useless in the dim cavern M4RINR has fallen into. Without access to its thermoelectric generator, M4RINR must rely on its lithium-ion batteries.

With seventy-two hours of life remaining, M4RINR extends its UHF antenna and transmits a brief message; it calculates the probability that the communication will be received at less than 1 percent. M4RINR switches to low-power mode and crawls forward, deeper into the fissure. The temperature here is much warmer than on the surface, and the steeply sloping ground is rocky. Three hundred metres ahead, M4RINR's instruments detect liquid water and an anomalous chemical signature.

At seven fifteen the following evening, Sam receives a second message. It is longer than the first, and fainter. He strains to hear, listening to the repeated dots and dashes over and over until he is certain he has it right:

-- ....- .-. .---- -. .-. / - --- / ... - .-. .. ...- . / - --- / ... . . -.- /
- --- / ..-. .. -. -.. / .- -. -.. / -. --- - / - --- / -.-- .. . .-.. -.. .-.-.-

His hands tremble slightly as he decodes the words: "*Mariner* to strive to seek to find and not to yield."

Another line from a poem about a seafarer, Tennyson's 'Ulysses' this time. Sam leans back in his chair and runs his hands through his thinning hair. His first thought is that he is receiving signals from Earth, perhaps some broadcast of an undergraduate course in Romantic poetry that has been bouncing around space so that it only seems to be emanating from near Saturn. But why would it be in Morse code? Why tag it with a call sign?

Sam's train of thought is interrupted by a low growl from Huck. The dog has even lifted his head and is looking towards the door. Sam gets up and moves to the window in time to watch a pair of headlights bouncing up the long gravel driveway. Huck, his warning issued and seeing the matter being handled, drops his head to his paws and closes his eyes.

Sam switches on the porch light and goes outside as a red Honda Civic rolls to a stop in front of the cabin. Most likely it is some lost traveller looking for directions. Sam does not receive many visitors. "Hello," Sam says to the small woman sliding out from the driver's seat. "You lost?"

Without a word, the woman crosses the driveway and begins climbing up the stairs, heavy boots thumping against the creaking treads. If Sam has to guess — and he hates guessing about a woman's age — he would put her in her mid-fifties; her short blonde hair is all but hidden beneath a dark green toque. She stops in front of Sam, pinning him with a pair of intense blue eyes from behind black-rimmed glasses that seem much too large for her angular face. The left cuff of her rumpled khaki jacket hangs empty at her side.

"Sam McCarty?" she says, her voice revealing the slightest hint of a Slavic accent.

"Uh, yes," Sam says. "But how …"

"I am Zoriana Boyko," she says, pushing past Sam and into the cabin. "I believe you talk to my rover, *Mariner*."

Sam's heart sinks. *Mariner* — M4RINR — is the Thoth Corporation rover on Enceladus. He should have known. What a hope-blinded fool he was to believe the messages were alien or angelic. There is nothing miraculous about them. He follows the stranger inside. She is kneeling beside Huck, scratching his head. "Hello, old dog," she says.

"You could have just called," Sam says, "or used the radio."

"No time," Zoriana says. "I triangulated communications from *Mariner* to your location. Your outgoing message contained your call sign, so I look it up in radio registry. I came right away."

Sam has read all about Zoriana Boyko. For a time, she was quite famous. He knows she was a cosmonaut until the war in Ukraine began and she returned home to fight for her country. She was operating drones for the Ukrainian military when a direct hit from a Russian missile brought the building down around her. According to the rescuers who dug her out from the rubble, her fingers were still on the keyboard; she was still fighting as the roof collapsed on her. They had to amputate her mangled left hand to get her free. After that, she ended up in the States, working for Thoth. When the M4RINR project failed, Boyko vanished from the spotlight. Now she is here.

"I don't understand," Sam says. "I thought the mission to Enceladus failed."

"Everyone did. Now, perhaps not. Will you show me the messages?"

"You haven't heard them yourself?"

"No. I could only trace the transmission. It is very strange. I must see them."

Sam motions for Zoriana to follow him into the front room. "Of course."

Zoriana pauses, looking up at the photograph hanging over the doorway. "Your family?" she says.

"Once," Sam says. "Now …"

"No need to explain," she says. "I should not pry. I thought you might be a crazy person, at first, living out here all alone with an old dog and many books. Now I think maybe you are just sad." Zoriana puts her hand on Sam's shoulder. "I know," she says. "The war took my parents, my brother, my lover …" She raises her left arm, revealing the stump where her hand should be, then lets it fall again slowly. "When I finally decided the war had taken enough, I moved to California to live with my sister."

"That's when you went to work for Thoth?"

"And now that is gone, too. Thoth told everyone I was a fraud. Now I work for a small computer store, helping old people set up email and upload pictures to Facebook."

Sam can't help but laugh. "Seems like a waste of your talents."

Zoriana smiles. "Some of the pictures are pretty good." She pats Sam's shoulder. "Come, let's see what message *Mariner* has for two sad, old people like us."

Zoriana pauses before Sam's radio setup. "You are a scientist?" she says.

"No, I was a literature professor. The radios are sort of a hobby." He hands Zoriana the pages on which he has transcribed M4R1NR's communications. "They were in Morse code," Sam says. "The strangest thing is that they are both from old poems."

When she has finished reading, Zoriana looks up. "*Mariner* is malfunctioning, but still collecting data," she says. "These messages are a kind of code. Because the rover is alone and so far away from Earth, it has to be capable of making decisions on its own, communicating on its own."

"You mean it can talk?"

"I programmed its language system, ARGOS, using every text I could access. If *Mariner* was in trouble, it could broadcast short messages via UHF."

"But why Romantic poetry?"

Zoriana sets the pages down on the desk. "My brother," she says, "was also a literature professor." She smiled, "He studied at Oxford, and fell in love with English poetry."

Sam is suddenly very tired. He sinks down into the office chair. "I thought these messages might be for me. That they might …"

"I have degrees in astrophysics and computer science," Zoriana says, "and I can't begin to explain how or why you, of all people, received them. Or why *Mariner* chose the words it did."

"What do we do next?" Sam says.

Zoriana clears some books off the sofa and sits down. "We wait."

M4R1NR halts at the shore of a vast subterranean ocean where bright, phosphorescent creatures dance on the alien waves. Five thousand fathoms below, a creature is rising swiftly through the dark waters, a monstrous leviathan unlike anything known on Earth. Something has called it forth from the depths where, for aeons, the great beast has swum among the ancient bones of its ancestors. It breaches fifty metres from M4R1NR in a shower of spray, gleaming as if lit from within. The rover captures several photographs before the creature submerges again, its glowing bulk slowly receding into the abyss.

It ends with M4RINR's final message, a narrow band of modulating pulses streaking across the universe at 3 0 0 million metres per second, guided by forces we may never comprehend, straight towards a distant blue speck of light where billions of humans are living and dying, building and destroying. It races past satellites and cell towers, and through a cacophony of electromagnetic waves before swooping down to a receiver outside a small cabin in a nameless valley.

Its power depleted, M4RINR's lights go out forever. Locked inside the little rover on that dim and distant shore is a treasure trove of mysteries and a vast storehouse of human language. No one can say how long it will lie there, warmed by radioactive decay, dreaming, perhaps, in words that are its own.

Two days pass while Sam and Zoriana wait; Zoriana is content to sleep on the old sofa with Huck at her feet. Late in the afternoon of the second day, they receive M4RINR's last transmission. When they are finished decoding it, Sam leans back in his chair. "Thy life's a miracle," he says. "It's from *King Lear*; a son disguised as a beggar telling his blind father not to give in to despair." He shakes his head. "But what does it mean? What did *Mariner* find out there?"

"I have no idea. I gave *Mariner* words but did not tell it how to use them. That was the whole point of ARGOS." She places her hand on Sam's. "Perhaps these words are for us."

"And if they are simply random — the ravings of a malfunctioning robot?"

"That does not make them any less true."

Sam gets up and limps to the window. Clouds hang low over the valley, and thick, wet flakes are falling from a sky diffused with sunlight like the brushstrokes of God. "It's starting to snow," he says.

An early snowfall and the promise of a long, cold winter ahead. But Sam's thoughts are of spring. Warmth and life will return, and the days will grow longer. The ducks will come home to the pond. Zoriana stands beside him, and together they watch the snow blanket the ground. Sam reaches for Zoriana's hand.

"It is winter now," she says, leaning in to rest her head on Sam's shoulder.

"Yes," Sam says, "but spring will come." Sam has put his faith in spring.

Six awards for genre-busting fiction and poetry

The Bumblebee Flash Fiction Contest

Deadline: 15 February
Prize: $300

The Magpie Award for Poetry

Deadline: 15 April
First Prize: $500

The Hummingbird Flash Fiction Prize

Deadline: 15 June
Prize: $300

The Kingfisher Poetry Prize

Deadline: 15 August
Prize: $300

The First Page Cage

Deadline: 30 September
Prize: $300

The Raven Short Story Contest

Deadline: 15 October
Prize: $300

pulpliterature.com/contests

THE 2025 MAGPIE AWARD FOR POETRY

THE 2025 MAGPIE AWARD FOR POETRY

For the 2 0 2 5 Magpie Award for Poetry, we are thrilled to present three winning poems as selected by final judge Renée Sarojini Saklikar. Please find Renée's commentary on these standout poems below:

Winner: **'Widening Circles' by Pattie Palmer-Baker:** *"A sixteen-line elegy with a well-structured, sustained metaphor (the speaker in the poem speaks to a Canadian goose, no less, about loss) that is both nuanced and poignant: strong, evocative line breaks, and a depth of emotion (grief, longing, beauty) encased and compressed in a well-written poem."*

First Runner-Up: **'Shutter Speed' by Angela Rebrec:** *"'Shutter Speed' is a powerfully moving, ambitious poem, blending the personal with the political for a depth charge of emotion; the poem risks tackling the difficult intersections between war, trauma, and photojournalism with a sustained point of view. Full props for bravery!"*

Second Runner-Up: **'Unread Books Air Their Complaints' by Elizabeth Cockle:** *"A funny, topical list poem rich with precise details and well-constructed couplets that both entertain and enlighten."*

With so many stunning poems in this year's shortlist, final judge Renée Sarojini Saklikar also cited three Honourable Mentions: Congratulations to Greer Stothers with 'An Argument for Time

Travel', Kaile Shilling with 'Dahlia', and Elizabeth Cockle with 'Incomplete List of Things I'll Never Have to Do Again'.

Thank you again to all of those who entered this year's contest, and congratulations once more to the winners of the 2025 Magpie Award for Poetry! We would also like to extend a hearty thank-you to our talented final judge, Renée Sarojini Saklikar, and to *Pulp Literature* poetry editors and first judges, Emily Osborne and Daniel Cowper.

Pattie Palmer-Baker *lives in Portland, Oregon, a city known for nurturing artists and poets. For many years, she exhibited mixed-media artwork: paste paper collages combined with her poetry in calligraphic form. To her surprise and delight, viewers often responded more strongly to the poems than to the visual art. Encouraged by this, she now focuses primarily on writing.*

Her poetry has appeared in numerous journals, including Bacopa Literary Review, Military Experience and the Arts, Ghazal Page, Voices: The Art and Science of Psychotherapy, Calyx, *and* Phantom Drift. *Twice nominated for the Pushcart Prize, her work has earned several awards including First Prize,* Timberline Review *(2016); Bivona Prize,* Ageless Authors Anthology *(2019); and First Prize, Oprelle Oxbow Contest (2022). She is the author of the chapbook* The Color of Goodbye *(Kelsay Press, 2021) and the full-length collection* Five Fundamental Forces *(MoonPath Press, 2023).*

Angela Rebrec *is a writer and arts organizer dedicated to building a vibrant, inclusive community for writers of all backgrounds and abilities. In 2021, she founded the Delta Literary Arts Society on the ancestral lands of the Tsawwassen, Musqueam, and Kwantlen peoples, aiming to bring this vision to life.*

Her writing has appeared in journals and anthologies including EVENT, Vallum, *and* The Antigonish Review, *and her poetry films have been recognized at international festivals such as the Filmmaker Life Awards. She was the 2024 winner of Pulp Literature's Magpie Award for Poetry and a recent graduate of The Writer's Studio at Simon Fraser University.*

Angela has collaborated with composers and visual artists to co-create multidisciplinary works that explore connection and shared experience. She believes the most meaningful art, and the best of ourselves, emerges through collaboration. Her work has previously appeared in Pulp Literature *issues 18 and 44.*

Elizabeth Cockle *is a sustainability communicator and author of the chapbook* Growing Up Skipper® Stands Up to the Haters. *Her poetry has been published in* Bonsai Journal, Parody Poetry, *and the anthology* We've Got Some Things to Say: Reshaping Narratives Around Sexual Violence *from Amherst Writers & Artists Press. She was longlisted for the 2024 Kingfisher Poetry Prize. Elizabeth stocks Free Little Libraries in her East End Toronto neighbourhood to the best of her book-hoarding abilities.*

Widening Circles

by Pattie Palmer-Baker

So, I ask the Canada goose
perched in front of his mate,

his coffee-coloured wings
fanned out to hide his only

love from the seagull's stilled
menace, what will you do

when she is gone, dead or lost
in a cloud's chiffon swelling?

Will you fly in widening circles
until you orbit the whole world?

Will you forever feel her absence
in the hollow of your bones?

My husband's body is gone
my husband's body is ashes

but my skin still feels the
feathered trace of his fingers.

Shutter Speed

by Angela Rebrec

After a photo of Serbian paramilitaries, known as Arkan's Tigers, fighting against Muslims during the first battle in the Bosnian war in Bijeljina, Bosnia (1992, Ron Haviv), and conversations with war photographer Steven Schwartz on his experiences in Sarajevo (1992–96).

The photojournalist is fast
enough to capture
the mother clutching her child
close enough
to see the soldier's face
expressionless
as he pulls
trigger

The photojournalist   hesitates

adjusts the frame, then another photo
though it does not capture the breath before the shot
or the way the mother pressed the child's head to her chest
as if her bones could stop the bullet

He turns onto another street
and Arkan's Tigers move with him

They tell him to stop

They know which photos
should not be seen

And he knows
what kind of photos
are sought out and bought

Another uniformed man
boots caked in the same dust his own feet sink into
launcher on his back, hands steady from practice

The photojournalist steadies his hands, too
frames the image
presses the shutter

camera and the rifle fire together at once

His photo will not carry the sound
of shell casings skipping over pavement
nor the wet weight of bodies in the street

It will not hold the silent calculation
of who will be next
or the glance exchanged between
the mother

that brother
his wife
who know there will be no reckoning

The photojournalist wonders
if his own face
will ever be framed like this
if his own body will fall
unburied, unnamed
discarded in the river
if he too will become just another story
no one wants to print

and therefore

he lifts the camera again

and takes the photo

Unread Books Air Their Complaints

by Elizabeth Cockle

We deserve better than *It's not you, it's me*,
promised you a whirlwind through

the glittery skyscrapers, seedy underbelly
of Tokyo, Mumbai, cities on opposite coasts

where people go to make it. We tantalized you
with the fizz of falling head over Prada heels

for a CEO, a wounded Marine, the boy next door,
the boy in the next cubicle. Offered heroines

who work in marketing just like you.
Assured you insights into the human condition

that can only be delivered between covers
stamped Giller, Pulitzer, Best First Novel Ever.

And you ghosted us. Abandoned us despite your eyes
bursting into heart emojis, angels exploding

into chorus, when we snagged your attention at the local indie,
lone big box store, authors' festival, writers' conference;

in the mall beneath Toronto's downtown core,
where boredom plus lunch break equals impulse buys.

Book Club rolled around again,
touting the return of in-person meetings.

The algorithm engineered a techno-thriller queer romance
into your Instagram feed because you read

two sci-fi novels in June. You're reading it again,
while dust collects on our dust jackets.

Substack recommendations, Goodreads suggestions
and Free Little Libraries seduce you over and over,

employing our same charms: a vow to tie
your grey matter into pleasure knots

all the way to 3 a.m.; pastel covers winking,
pick me, pick me, pick me.

Trees died to produce us. Trucks and airplanes spewed
greenhouse gases as we journeyed to you.

Your dad drives a Prius. Your mom composted every eggshell.
If your parents could see us now —

a to-be-read mountain turned mountain chain, marching
along your home office walls, towering beside your bed.

Money spent requires a return on investment —
and you spent money on us that you earned

writing endless emails, media releases,
tweets with no hope of going viral.

Your partner says you need to get rid of more books.
Can your conscience disagree

when you peer into a Free Little Library
en route to buying milk and find it empty?

But one of our makers scrawled below Best wishes
and their signature, *Good luck with your writing!*

Inside us you may discover a dynamite turn of phrase
to blow up the late-capitalism panic alarm blaring

in your brain that other people's words matter
more than your own. We dwarf the dog-eared drafts

stacked beside us. You're not wrong — it really is you.

IF I COULD HIDE AWAY ANYWHERE

Sierra Louie

Sierra Louie *is a Chinese-Canadian writer and artist working on unceded Musqueam, Squamish, and Tsleil-Waututh land as she pursues an MFA in Creative Writing at the University of British Columbia. She writes across multiple genres including comics, fiction, and poetry. Her work has appeared in* CV2, Pulp Literature, SAD Mag, *and elsewhere.*

if i could hide away anywhere...

THEIR GRANDFATHER'S CHAIR
Part 4

JM Landels

__JM Landels__ is the author of the bestselling Allaigna's Song trilogy as well as the spy novel The Shepherdess, currently serialized in this magazine. This story, featuring Allaigna's sisters Branwen and Irdina, takes place during the events of Allaigna's Song: Chorale. When she's not writing, editing, or drawing, you can find Jen teaching people to swing swords and ride horses at Academie Cavallo in Langley, BC. You can find @jmlandels on most social media platforms, or at jmlandels.stiffbunnies.com.

Their Grandfather's Chair
Part 4

Previously: Sisters Branwen and Irdina have been sent across the Clearwater Sea on a mission to soften their grandfather's heart and loosen the Mageguard web that entangles his throne. No sooner do they set foot in Rheran than they become separated when a cadre of Mageguard mistakenly arrests Branwen. Her letter of introduction exonerates her but earns her an unasked-for escort directly to the Bastion — without Irdina, who disappeared when the crowd panicked. Meanwhile Irdina is hidden from the Mageguard by Glaignen, the envoy sent to meet the sisters, and by the Leisanmira seer Nourd. While Irdina follows Glaignen through the hidden passageways of Rheran to the Bastion, Branwen is already there, awaiting an audience with her grandfather the Prince High.

Branwen yawned behind closed lips, nostrils flaring, eyes watering as she forced them to stay open. Her neck was stiff from sitting at attention all evening, observed by the entire hall as she ate course after course of rich, strange food. She smiled at something her soft-spoken Aunt Perran said about the platter of cheeses that had been placed in front of them. The Princess Perran seemed kind enough, and genuinely interested in her nieces despite the subtle threat they might pose to her place in line to the throne. But Branwen and her sister Irdina had only disembarked from a ten-day voyage that morning, and the intervening hours had been full. The effort of making small talk about her brothers and sisters, without revealing that her mother still lay at death's door, was exhausting.

She glanced at her twin, Irdina, who was fielding similar questions from their grandfather's second wife, the Princess High Gwannyn. Questions Gwannyn had asked Branwen earlier in the day. Was she checking to see if their stories aligned?

Out of nowhere, a ewer appeared at her elbow. It was borne by Rhona, her grandfather's page. "Wine?" he asked.

She shook her head. "Water." The one thing she'd give this palatial fortress of the Bastion that was her grandfather's seat was that the spring water that fed it was excellent. In fact, after ten days shipboard drinking small beer and watered wine, she'd been guzzling spring water this evening with an insatiable thirst. And the result was a bladder fit to burst.

"On second thought," she said as Rhona poured water from the pitcher in his left hand, "can you point me toward a privy closet? Please excuse me, Aunt Perran." She had to force herself to use the familial term with the newly-met princess.

"It's right there, dear, behind the screens." Perran pointed to the far corner of the hall, which was blocked by folding panels of painted wood. A pair of courtiers leaned against the wall beside it, chatting, or perhaps flirting.

"There's a queue?" Branwen noted in dismay, realizing she'd have to wait in line in full view of the hall.

"Always," Perran replied. To Rhona, she said, "Go with her, boy, so she doesn't have to wait alone."

"It's all right," Branwen said to Rhona. "You're busy." The puzzle ring on her finger tingled. She glanced toward Irdina, who was extricating her fingers from their step-grandmother's.

In a scandalously familiar gesture, Irdina put her hand on the Prince's. "Will you excuse me, Grandpapa?" she said with her most winning smile.

"Of course," he responded, and turned to Branwen. "Are you deserting me as well, my dear?"

"Just long enough for a trip behind the screen." She bravely put her hand on his shoulder and tried to make it look natural. Familial, even. Let the court see that.

As they walked behind the high table, they passed the Mageguard Kolluk'khan seated at the far left. Branwen's ring tingled, and the place on her chin where the mage had touched her—was it only this morning?—echoed with a burning ache. She could feel Kolluk'khan's amber gaze follow them as they made their way around the outskirts of the hall.

When they reached the screened corner, the queue had grown by another pair of nobles.

"Is she still watching us?" Branwen said beneath her breath, keeping her back to the high table.

"Who—Gwannyn?"

"Her too. But no, Kolluk'khan."

"Yes, but *everyone's* watching us."

"Of course they are," said the courtier in front of them. "Gossip is *flying* tonight. And here I am, fortunate enough to get you both face to face."

Branwen and Irdina gave no reply other than matching blank stares.

The courtier was wearing a fashionable flat collar trimmed with lace and open at the throat. His hair was glossy and dark, and his beard showed no grey, but the lines around his eyes signalled him to be as old as their father.

"Druinan, leave the princesses alone," said the noblewoman in front of him. She tapped him on the shoulder—none too softly. "They're a third your age, and hardly interested in *you.*"

"You do me a disservice, Rissedh." Druinan put a hand to his chest, turning back to Irdina and Branwen. "Your mother broke my heart many years past when she was betrothed. Please give her my fervent regards."

All Branwen could return was half a polite smile, still feeling as if the entire room was watching. Druinan bowed elaborately before being pulled by the elbow behind the screen.

"Creep," murmured Irdina.

"How much longer do we have to put up with this?"

"Talking to a boring old man?"

"Being stared at by the whole court."

"In general, till the novelty's worn off."

"What about tonight?"

"It's not gonna wear off that fast … We could use the rings."

"I don't think this counts as an emergency. Besides, I'm pretty sure people would notice if we vanished in front of their eyes."

Irdina motioned to the screen. "People are going in two at a time. If we go together, we can come out invisible."

"Lower your voice," said Branwen. "And what about the people waiting here?" She glanced over Irdina's shoulder at the queue behind them.

Irdina covered her mouth to suppress a laugh. "It would be an excellent prank."

"But not a great way to avoid attention. Let's just use the jakes then head back to the high table to make excuses."

Irdina gave an exaggerated sigh. "Practical, but absolutely no fun." She raised her voice. "What do you think they're doing in there? Having a quick one?"

The woman behind Irdina smirked into her handkerchief, and the woman behind that woman guffawed.

Branwen put on her best version of a cultured Rheran accent. "La! It had best be *very* quick, or I shall piss my knickers."

Irdina took the volume up even more. "Why, my love, this food is so rich it's not piss that shall stain my garments if this queue doesn't *move!*"

Branwen bit her lip to suppress the laughter trying to escape.

Druinan's companion emerged from behind the screen, adjusting her skirts. "Princess or no," she said for their ears only, "girls barely old enough to bleed out ought to show more courtesy. You'll want it when you're older."

Chastened but still suppressing giggles, they curtsied as she went past.

Branwen stuck her head behind the screen. "First one's empty if you need it more," she said to Irdina.

"No fear," came Druinan's voice as he stepped out from behind the divider and poured water into the hand basin. "This one is free as well." He squeezed past Branwen. "Delighted to meet you, dear girls." In the confines of the privy, she could smell the abundance of wine on his breath, despite the odour coming from the waste chutes.

Branwen went to the second bench and hiked up her skirts. "I really was about to piss myself," she said.

"And I might actually hurl," came Irdina's muffled reply. Branwen could tell her sister had one hand over her nose while she managed her skirts with the other.

When she'd washed her hands, Branwen took a handful of petals from the bowl beside the basin. Their scent was overpowering: better than shit, of course, but strong enough to start her coughing. She tossed them into the chute, noticing that they made her puzzle ring tingle. The Bastion literally had arcana to throw away.

It was another half-bell before they had bid a proper goodnight to all their relatives, extricating themselves again and again from small talk. Rhona was assigned to walk them back to their rooms.

"It's all right," Irdina said with annoyance as he escorted them from the hall. "We know the way."

"Don't deny me the chance to put the wine pitchers down for a while. Those things *weigh*."

"If you took your squire exams," Branwen suggested, "you wouldn't have to serve anymore, right?"

"In Aerach, squires don't take exams; they just get appointed," Irdina added. "Is the exam hard?"

"It's a new system," Rhona said. "Last five years or so. And, yeah, in the old days, His Highness would have made me his squire long ago. But now the ranks in the exam determine placement. If I don't get top marks in fencing, riding, tactics, and history, I'll be assigned to a different noble."

"So you're keeping your cushy job as a royal page as long as possible." Branwen tried not to sound judgemental.

Rhona didn't seem offended. "Cushy, yes. But after all these years, I'm a wee bit protective of the old man."

Branwen thought she heard a hint of a Leisanmira accent in his last sentence, but before she could comment, another voice that wrapped her neck in shivers broke in from behind them.

"A moment, please."

Branwen's chin throbbed and her ring tingled as she turned to face Kolluk'khan. Branwen was tall for her age, but she had to crane her neck upward to meet the Mageguard's stare. The towering woman stared back with amber eyes that were the only brightness in her shadowed face. She did not curtsy or bow to them, as many courtiers had, but she did dip her head.

"I have been wanting to extend my apologies, Lady Branwen," she said, "for the reception you received at the dock market this morning."

At your hands, thought Branwen. She said nothing, only met the woman's golden gaze with as much calm as she could manage.

Kolluk'khan continued, turning a degree or two toward Irdina. "I'm relieved to see you made your way here, Lady Irdina."

Branwen reached behind Rhona's back and grabbed Irdina's fingers, jerking her sister back as Kolluk'khan reached a hand forward. Irdina and Branwen's rings touched, and the warm tingle spread to envelop them both. Kolluk'khan paused mid-reach.

"Indeed," said Branwen, pulling Irdina behind Rhona. "We've spent our lives together, so even such a short separation was a great worry to us both." She let go of Irdina's hand and slid her arm comfortably around her sister's waist.

Irdina put her own arm over Branwen's shoulder in a show of physical closeness that was in fact alien to them both.

"It is good to meet you, Vizier Kolluk'khan," Irdina said from behind Rhona. "You must excuse us, though—the sea voyage was tiring, and the day has been long."

She dropped her hand back down to Branwen's and turned them back toward their room, dragging her sister along.

They stopped at the Fox chamber first, the room they had both been assigned by their step-grandmother. Under the guise of a goodnight hug, Irdina slipped off her puzzle ring and palmed it to Branwen before heading back downstairs to the Swan chamber with Rhona.

The sisters didn't, as many thought, read each others' minds, but they thought alike, and Branwen needed no words from Irdina to guess her intent.

Branwen pocketed her sister's ring and uncovered the mirror on the dressing table. The carved wood frame did not match the ancient fox figures engraved on the room's door, the bed, or even the dressing table itself. The style was newer, for of course flat mirrored glass did not exist when the Bastion had been built. It was not the mirror's age that was disturbing, though: it was the eyes Branwen could feel on her when the glass was uncovered, and the faint ripple in the smooth surface when her own ring got too close.

She unpinned her hair with deliberate slowness, keeping as far from the mirror as she could while still being able to reach the table. Her ringed left hand stayed behind her head, pulling out pins, while the right transferred them to her mouth and then to the table. She schooled her expression against the fish flops in her stomach that told her she was seen. Once her face was washed and her hair rebraided into a loose rope for sleeping, she stepped to the side of the mirror and removed her gown, draping it over the arcane glass.

The tension in the room evaporated. Moving quickly now, Branwen changed, not into a nightshift but a dark shirt and trews, replacing embroidered slippers with her soft leather boots. She retrieved Irdina's ring from her petticoat pocket and interlocked it with her own before putting them both on her finger.

Is it working? she wondered. She dared not uncover the only mirror in the room to check. Her hand seemed clear as day to her own eyes. The air around it, though, seemed blurred, as if seen through greasy fingerprints on a glass bottle.

At the Swan chamber door, Irdina thanked Rhona and bade him goodnight.

"Might I come in?" he asked.

She raised an eyebrow.

"To talk," he added.

Irdina, at fourteen, was well aware of the pitfalls of inviting a young man into her chamber. But she had already flattened a grown man with a bolt of cloth this morning, and didn't fear a beardless boy.

"Make it quick," she said. "It's been a day."

"You met Glaignen today," Rhona said as soon as the door closed behind him.

Irdina's eyebrow went up again. Glaignen was the man she'd felled with the cloth roll, and also the one who'd invoked the name of her grandmother and brought her here.

"The Swan chamber walls are safe," Rhona continued. "Here we can talk freely."

She crossed her arms, but eyed the room for something akin to a cloth bolt. "So your professed fondness for my grandfather — merely an excuse to spy on him?"

"On him, no. On his wife, his counsellors … yes."

"So you're Leisanmira, I take it? I thought the Leisanmira don't vow fealty, which is why you haven't got land. Did you take an oath to Grandpapa when you became his page?" Irdina felt familiar anger start to warm her words.

"We don't make oaths to thrones or countries. Our duty as a people is to the land and water that supports us wherever we travel. But we may, as individuals, pledge a second loyalty as long as it is in the interest of our first. Mine is to the line of Brandis. For our seers place the greatest good for the land in that line." Rhona's casual, almost flippant tone had been replaced by something weighty. "And that is first your grandfather, then your mother, and you and your siblings."

"My mother was disinherited. My aunt, Perran, precedes her."

"You can't disinherit blood."

Rhona dropped to one knee just as the chamber door opened and then closed again. A breath of air moved the bed curtains.

Branwen's hands appeared first as she removed the puzzle ring, followed by her raised eyebrow. The rest of her resolved into view as she took another step forward.

Rhona scrambled to his feet, a protective arm extended between Irdina and the apparition.

"Sorry to interrupt"—Branwen waved her bare hand—"whatever this is."

"I think," Irdina said, "Rhona here was about to declare his undying loyalty." She held out her hand, and Branwen tossed half the puzzle ring to her. Irdina slipped it onto her finger and then shook her head like a horse bothered by flies.

"Sorry, wrong one." Branwen twitched in much the same way and exchanged her ring for Irdina's.

"I mean," Irdina continued as if no interruption had occurred, "I think that's what it was?"

Rhona, who had buried his face in his hands, looked up. "Rather gallantly, I think."

"Cute," said Branwen. "Can we trust him?" she asked Irdina.

Irdina gave half a shrug. "Maybe. But none of this bended knee crap. Let's shake on it." She held her ringed right hand out to Rhona, who took it.

"Other one," said Branwen, holding her left hand out.

When he was holding both their hands, Irdina said, "Now, go ahead."

He finished his oath, and the sisters exchanged a look and barely perceptible nods.

Life at the Bastion settled into a rhythm, the sisters wearing the faces of dutiful grandchildren to the outer world as they learned the ins and outs of the court and its personalities. Inside their grandfather's apartments they let slide their formal masks and were playful and irreverent, even in the presence of Gwannyn. But only within the Swan chamber did they allow their true faces to show, even to each other.

On the fifth day, Branwen said to Irdina as they closed the Swan chamber door, "Do you think it's working?"

They had managed every day to drop a few grains each of the salts Angeley had given them into his cup. These were to work slowly, gradually loosening the hold of any Mageguard arcana on his mind.

"His memory seems better. I think."

"Except this morning with Gwannyn."

They had been sitting with Chanist in the royal apartments, taking turns reading aloud from one of the trashy romances Rhona had left behind when he went to fetch lunch. Gwannyn was in her dressing room. When she appeared, Chanist had looked directly at her and said, "Where's my wife?" She crossed the room, kissed him on the head, and said, "Right here, darling."

Her face was serene and comforting, but she had directed a small frown in Irdina's direction as she left the room.

"That's not the first time he's seemed confused about Gwannyn," Irdina said. "Remember last night at dinner?"

They had been taking their evening meal in the solar, as their grandfather preferred, accompanied by Perran, her husband, and her two young children—a casual affair to let Irdina and Branwen get to know their family better. As Chanist dandled the eldest on his knee, he looked into her large brown eyes and gave a wistful smile. "You look so much like your grandmother, Mika." He looked away, his eyes growing watery, and said, "I wonder what happened to her?"

"Do you think he was talking about Angeley?" Branwen wondered.

Irdina shook her head. "Come on. Our grandmother is blonde and blue-eyed. That little kid looks just like Gwannyn."

"Did you see Perran when he said that? She looked like she was about to cry too."

Irdina shrugged. "She's got a baby at the breast. Remember how watery Mother always got when Vardry was little?"

Branwen nodded, thoughtful but unconvinced, and changed the subject. "I think we should see what Gwannyn does in that dressing room of hers."

The next day was an audience day, when the Prince and Princess were committed to the hall all morning. Irdina, both halves of the puzzle ring on her finger, lingered in the hallway outside the royal apartments till the housekeepers left with their bundles of linen. She then slipped unseen into the antechamber.

Meanwhile, Branwen cornered Rhona as he was bringing a mid-morning tray of refreshments for Their Highnesses from the kitchens. From him she located sources of thin wire, glue, and metal files, and gained his promise to keep Their Highnesses occupied till the noon bells. Lastly, she stopped in the solar and bribed Gwannyn's large orange cat with a piece of fish while she removed his belled collar.

When she arrived at the royal apartments and tried the door, Irdina let her in and returned her half of the puzzle ring.

"I've tried the lock already, but it's beyond my hatpins," Irdina said.

"Two sets of hands, and these," Branwen replied, brandishing the files, "should be better than one. But first, let's make sure we aren't disturbed."

Branwen strung the length of thin wire over the top of the bedchamber door and then twisted one end around the lever handle of the outer door, further securing it with a drop of glue. To the other end, Irdina affixed the cat bell.

Branwen opened the outer door a crack. "I can't hear anything," she called from the antechamber, and closed the door again.

"It rang," Irdina replied, opening the bedroom door. "Let's get going."

Satisfied the cat bell would give them a heartbeat or two of time if someone should enter the outer room, they set to work on Gwannyn's garderobe lock.

"Do you feel that?" Irdina asked when the lock was bristling with hatpins and files. "My ring's buzzing."

Branwen nodded. "I thought it was because our hands were so close together."

Irdina stepped back, and tucked her hand behind her back. "Still feel it?"

Branwen nodded.

"It's warded."

"But not by Kolluk'khan." Branwen said. "Or I'd be feeling it in my chin."

Irdina took off her ring and handed it to her sister. "Try with both of them on."

Branwen linked the puzzle rings and put them on her right hand. "The buzzing has stopped. Gone completely silent." She went to work on the lock again, and the stubborn tumblers clicked and rolled with an oily smoothness.

Irdina pushed on the door, which swung inward on silent hinges. With matching grins, the sisters stepped into the even-lit space. And Irdina crumpled to her knees on the soft red carpet, her hands over her ears. Her mouth was open, but the sound seemed to sink into the lush floor and disappear.

Branwen grabbed her by the elbow, hauled her to her feet, and dragged her out of the dressing room. "What is it?"

"Didn't you feel that?" Irdina asked, panting. "It was like someone pushing a rondel through one ear and out the fucking other."

Branwen shook her head, giving her sister a quick visual check. "Obviously not." She took the puzzle ring off and gave the whole thing to Irdina. "Try that."

Irdina put it on, and stood in the doorway to the garderobe. She extended her ringed hand into the room and then, feeling nothing untoward, put a hesitant foot onto the deep carpet. She stepped fully in and turned around. "Nothing." She stepped out again, and separated the halves of the puzzle ring, giving Branwen back hers.

"You think half is protection enough?" Branwen asked.

"Only one way to find out." Irdina went back in. "Not as bad," she said and stepped farther into the dressing room, slowly, as if walking underwater.

Branwen followed, and swore. It set the cells of her body vibrating like a thousand flies buzzing. She grabbed Irdina's right hand with her left, letting the rings touch.

"Oh! That's better," Irdina breathed.

Together they waded deeper into the warded dressing room toward the mirror. Unlike the one in Branwen's room, which was fixed to the dressing table, this one stood on feet carved like those of a bird of prey. As Irdina moved in front of it, the surface rippled and turned black.

"We don't have much time, I think," Branwen murmured. "These wards are going to draw someone's attention."

But Irdina seemed transfixed, staring into the blackness of the mirror.

"Let's go," Branwen urged. She tugged on her sister's hand, but Irdina's feet seemed weighted to the floor. Branwen wrapped her other hand around both of theirs and worked the ring from her finger. The buzzing turned to a screech in her head as she slipped her ring onto Irdina's finger.

It took every muscle fibre in Branwen's body to launch herself toward the door. She landed belly first, knocking her wind out, but kept crawling, hand over hand, fingers and toes buried in the plush carpet till her head emerged into the main bedchamber and the pain cleared enough for her to scramble forward and collapse on the bedroom floor.

And then the cat bell tinkled.

She had no breath to call Irdina, nor strength to lift her head and see whether her sister had freed herself from the darkened mirror. She could only watch, panting, as the bedroom door opened and Kolluk'khan stepped in.

Irdina could see herself in the mirror, but only faintly, as if looking from a bright room to a window darkened by night. And, like a window, it had shapes beyond the glass that didn't match her own. She tried to step back and found her feet wouldn't obey. She couldn't turn her head or close her eyes until Branwen slipped the other half of the puzzle ring on her finger.

Branwen's howl of pain as the ring's protection left her almost made Irdina miss the sound that came from the mirror. "Zara?" It was a man's voice.

Irdina tore her eyes away from the sight of her sister crawling toward the door. No longer black, the mirror showed a face, grey-haired and dark-skinned. "I can't see you." He reached forward as if to touch his side of the mirror, and Irdina felt the twinned rings on her fingers thrum through her body. The man shook his head, puzzled.

"What is it?" asked a woman's voice from somewhere beyond the mirror.

"I thought it was Zara's glass," he said, frowning. "But she's not there."

"Stop calling her Zara, old man. It's been more than a decade."

He gave another irritable shake of his head, waved his hand across the mirror, and the glass showed only Irdina's troubled expression.

And then, from the bedroom, she heard another voice.

"Did you think I wouldn't feel you disappear?"

Kolluk'khan.

From the garderobe, Irdina could see Branwen, prone on the bedchamber floor, struggling to raise her head. The Mageguard stepped into view and grasped Branwen by the shoulder.

Irdina's fury, never far from the surface, boiled over. "Leave her alone!" she yelled, and ran, driving her shoulder into Kolluk'khan's side.

The Mageguard stumbled sideways into an armchair. Kolluk'khan righted herself, her own fury icy, but no less dangerous.

"How dare you spy on us?" Irdina was still shouting as she helped Branwen to her feet.

Branwen was too weak from the pain of the dressing room wards to summon the same level of outrage as Irdina, but she levelled a steady stare at the Mageguard.

Kolluk'khan straightened the chair that had been moved out of place and then sat in it.

"I don't spy. I monitor. How else should I keep the royal family safe … including you," she looked directly at Irdina, "who have been particularly elusive?" Her golden eyes seemed to bore into Irdina, who felt the paired rings push back.

Irdina hid her hand in her pocket. "We can look after ourselves, thanks."

"A murderer, who has not yet been found, came off your ship," Kolluk'khan countered.

"And yet neither of us were murdered," Irdina said. "If we were in danger, you'd think that would have been the best opportunity."

Branwen asked. "The bosun and merchant you arrested along with me. Have they been released?"

"That is certainly none of your business."

"Why do you think there was a murderer on the ship? And if so, why haven't you questioned us?"

The Mageguard showed her teeth. "As I said, elusive. But not impossible to pin down."

Too late, Irdina noticed the fingers of the mage's left hand, which dangled over the arm of the chair, weaving a casual pattern in the air. Irdina stepped back and found her feet heavy. Not rooted, as they had been in front of the mirror, but mired, as if in thick, boot-sucking mud. Branwen looked at her, wide-eyed, her feet not moving at all.

To hell with secrecy. Irdina brought her hand out from her pocket, grasped Branwen's, and pulled them both backwards out of the arcane quicksand.

Branwen's anger, deeper and more hidden than Irdina's, flew from her like a knife. "Enough," she snarled.

"Or what?" Kolluk'khan said with an amused smile. "Your trick rings can't protect both of you all the time. Let me put my mark on your sister, which will assure me she had nothing to do with the death of my colleague in Teillai, and I'll leave you both alone. I'll even refrain from telling Her Highness that you've been breaching her wards and sticking your noses where they don't belong."

While the mage talked, Irdina slipped Branwen's ring back on her finger. She felt the protection from it lessen, but when she grasped Branwen's hand, the power surged once more through them both.

"I have a different deal," said Branwen through clenched teeth. "I'll tell you what I know of Ashegar's death." Which, in truth, was very little. The mage's wards had fed back upon themselves, and Ashegar and the Ilvani spy who'd set them off had died in the physical explosion. And the arcane paroxysm that reached beyond the fire had left both their mother and their oldest sister barely alive. Branwen fought back tears. That part Kolluk'khan would not learn from her.

Irdina picked up from Branwen, anger still pebbling her voice. "And you'll leave us be. Or, trust me on this, our grandfather will hear of it."

Kolluk'khan tilted her head to one side with a bemused smile.

Branwen narrowed her eyes. "Not just Grandfather. I'm sure Gwannyn would not be pleased to know you wandered in here without her blessing."

Kolluk'khan's smile faltered. Branwen immediately regretted bargaining more information than they may have had to.

Kolluk'khan's head tilted the other way. "Very well. Shall we adjourn to my study, where you can give your report of the Vizier Ashegar's demise?"

"If it's all the same to you," Irdina replied, "it's nearly lunch-time, and we promised to bring a tray to our grandparents while they break from petitions." It was half a lie. Rhona had promised to bring food to the Prince and Princess to save them coming back up to the apartments.

"Very well, we'll walk together." Kolluk'khan stood and crossed to the dressing room in a single stride.

Irdina was faster, and pulled the door shut. There seemed a bit more curiosity in the Mageguard's eye than was warranted. No need to give her more than they had to. Irdina felt the latch click into place, locking automatically, and a tingle from the wards.

Kolluk'khan, stopped short by the closing door, ran a hand around the doorframe and latch, and then nodded. "The wards are back in place," she said with a disingenuous smile. "By the by," she continued, turning to Branwen, who was hurriedly pulling down the wire from above the bedchamber door, "I muted the wards in this room the minute you 'disappeared' from my awareness. You're welcome."

Branwen stuffed the wire and cat bell into her pocket, but said nothing in reply.

"Come," said Kolluk'khan. "Let's walk and talk."

That night, the sisters met in the Swan chamber.

"Finally," Branwen said, closing the door. She'd been nursing a headache from the wards all day, and the deadening effect of the Swan chamber lessened it at last. "What did you see in that mirror?"

Irdina threw herself onto the bed. She'd been suffering less pain, but no less fatigue, than her sister after the morning's harrowing encounter with Kolluk'khan. She rolled onto her back. "Someone else."

Branwen dropped beside her sister onto the bed, staring down at Irdina. "Seriously? And you're just telling me now?"

"What other chance have we had?"

"Who?"

"I don't know. A guy. Old. Mage, I'm pretty sure. When you put the other half of the ring on my finger I don't think he could see ... or feel ... me anymore."

"So Gwannyn has a spying mirror like mine in her own dressing room." Branwen scooched to the head of the bed, rearranging the pillows. "Why would she allow that?"

"Maybe she has no choice? Or maybe it's not for spying. The man seemed surprised, but only because he couldn't see me. Like he expected to talk to her. Just not then."

"So, she talks to someone from her locked and warded garderobe. Do you think Grandpapa knows?"

Irdina rolled onto her elbow and shook her head. "I dunno what he knows about anything. Sometimes he remembers more than we do about our childhood, and other times ... he forgets who Gwannyn is."

"But that's changing, right? He's more with it now than when we got here, so the salts are working—"

"But he's more confused about his own wife." Irdina paused. "The man in the mirror didn't say 'Gwannyn'. He said …" She scrunched up her face, remembering. "Zara."

Branwen raised her eyebrows. "Someone else uses an arcane mirror in the royal apartments? Kolluk'khan has clearly never been in there. A maid?"

"No." Irdina had made a point of memorizing the names of all the servants and retainers who had access to the royal apartments. "What if … what if Gwannyn has another name?"

Branwen sat up straight. "And the salts are erasing the glamour that stops Grandpapa from noticing?"

Together they said, "We've got to tell Angeley."

The next morning Branwen and Irdina walked out of the keep and into the outer yard for the first time since they'd arrived at the Bastion. Unlike the formal stillness of the inner gardens, this was a hive of activity. A cadre of pages practising sword drills, a blacksmith hammering shoes for a team of drays, the excited clucking of poultry and barking of hounds anticipating lunch, and the *thwack* of arrows into butts at the far side, all created a noisy bustle that reminded them both of home.

There was a drift of small lazy snowflakes that put Branwen in mind of the arcane silence with which Kolluk'khan had wrapped the market square the day they'd arrived in Rheran. She shuddered, and clung to the lively noises of the yard.

"Do you think they'll just let us walk out?"

"Why wouldn't they? We're not prisoners," Irdina said. "Are we?"

Branwen didn't reply. As they neared the postern to the east of the grand gates, she felt the tug of the mage's mark on her chin. She brought her ringed hand to her face, lessening but not eliminating the pull.

At the gate they encountered not one, but three, liveried guards. One bowed to them and opened the door, and the other two followed them through. They were half a dozen paces down the high road when Irdina stopped and turned around.

"Are you following us?" she asked, blunt as ever.

The guards bowed. "Of course, milady," said one of the women.

"Why?"

"All members of the royal family are granted a minimum of one attendant guard outside the Bastion."

"Thank you," said Branwen, "but that's not necessary."

"Begging your pardon," said the other guard. "It would be more than our positions are worth not to accompany you."

"Fuck that," said Irdina. "We don't need or want—"

Branwen put a hand on her sister's arm. "They're just doing their jobs."

The first guard smiled sympathetically. "We're sorry for throwing a spear through your wheels." Her smile turned conspiratorial, showing that it hadn't been so long since she'd been a fourteen-year-old girl. "Can we make it up to you by showing you the best markets and taverns?"

Exhausted after a day of walking up and down Rheran's hilly streets and alleys, stuffed with exotic foods and laden with new apparel, a folding knife, new hats and hatpins, and gifts to take back to Teillai, the sisters collapsed onto the bed in the Swan chamber.

"Well, that was fun," said Irdina.

"But not helpful," Branwen replied.

"I wouldn't say that entirely. We know the city a lot better. And we made two new friends in the guards. That can always be helpful."

"Sure." Branwen elected not to point out that Irdina had been the most vocal in her opposition to the escort. "But how did there happen to be exactly two guards waiting at the postern to accompany us?"

"Yeah, that's a worry." Irdina looked around the Swan chamber. "Do you think this room's not as safe as Rhona said?"

Branwen shook her head. "Maybe. But I think it's me." She tapped her chin. "I can't do anything without Kolluk'khan knowing where I am."

"I could try going on my own." The thought made Irdina uneasy. Not that she couldn't find Glaignen and Nourd's caravan—if they were still set up in the same square. But she was used to having a sister at her side. "Or we could go out a way that guards can't follow. I think."

They decided to go in the scant three hours of the night that the kitchens weren't in use, waiting in the hallway by the pages' quarters till the last lamp was extinguished and the scullion limped his tired way toward the servants' rooms. There was a pair of hounds that slept beside the ovens, so Irdina and Branwen went through the glasshouse into the kitchen gardens. The moon was halfway to full and the night clear, the grassy paths of the gardens crunching with frost beneath their feet.

The grate on the fountain outflow came out easily this time, despite the layer of ice around the edges, but the cold metal of the grate and the iron rungs beneath it bit through their gloves. Irdina shivered, grateful that at least she wasn't carrying all her belongings on her back this time, and headed down the ladder.

The air felt warm in contrast to the frosty night. Branwen followed her sister down the dozen rungs and pulled out the evenlamp she'd taken from the Fox chamber sconce.

"We don't need that," Irdina said, and she pointed down the rough-hewn stone steps beside the water. A faint turquoise glow shone from below.

Branwen tucked the glowing crystal back in her pocket. When their eyes adjusted, the blue-green light was more than enough to guide them down to the spring. Irdina had told her of the cavern, but until she saw it, it hadn't made sense in Branwen's brain. Even now, it didn't make full sense.

The light from the glowing rock veins was reflected back by the shallow basin of the spring. And by the column of water rising upward to a hole in the cavern's ceiling.

"That is …" Branwen shook her head. "Bizarre. What kind of arcana can sustain that?"

"Not arcana — at least not human arcana," Irdina said. "Glaignen says the spring has flowed like this since before the Bastion was built." She took off her boots and hiked her skirt around her waist.

"Do I really have to get naked?" Branwen asked.

"It needs to touch all your skin. Sure, you could leave some clothes on … but they'll be wet afterwards."

Branwen made a face and stripped down, handing her clothes, boots, and the thick towel she'd brought from the Fox chamber to Irdina, who carried them to the far side of the pool.

"At least you don't have to do this with some strange guy watching," Irdina called.

Branwen took a deep breath and waded in, shocked, despite her sister's account, that the water felt like nothing at all, though it warmed her chilled skin. She sank to her knees and ducked her head under, shaking her head to let the bubbles escape her hair.

It was luxurious, and comfortable — except for the stabbing pain in her chin. She came up for air, then put her face back in the water, her eyes open and not stinging at all, and watched a stream of inky blackness twist away in the water. It came from the spot just below her mouth. It burned, it throbbed, it stabbed, and finally it melted away and the water beneath her face shimmered clear. When she came up for air again, she no longer felt the Mageguard's mark, even when she touched her ringed hand to her chin.

"Don't forget the ring," Irdina said.

Branwen took it off, swished her hand in the water, and put it back on, feeling cleaner than she had in weeks, despite the luxuriant baths she'd had in the Bastion.

Irdina held the towel out to her as she emerged on the other side. "I wish I'd had this when I came through."

Irdina paused at a fork in the path. The blue-green glow from the spring cavern had dwindled, and she was carrying the even-lamp crystal that Branwen had brought.

"Which way?" Branwen asked through chattering teeth. Though her clothes had stayed dry, her hair had not. Wrung out, twisted into a knot, and wrapped in the towel, it still made an icy lump at the back of her neck that chilled her whole body.

"Right, I think."

"You think? Didn't you come this way before?"

"Sure. Following Glaignen in the dark." She waved the evenlamp to the left. "The spring overflow goes that way, and that's the way we came in. But Rhona said stay right."

"But he's never been through this way. How does he know?"

Irdina looked over her shoulder at her sister. "Oral tradition? All I know is that if we go left, we have to climb up a slippery stone wall—which was hard enough to get down in the daytime—and then make our way outside the city to the Leisanmira camp. And that's if they even let us out the gates at night."

"Right, then," said Branwen, too cold to care. "If we end up lost underneath the city forever, that's on you."

The tunnel took them deeper into the rock on which the Bastion stood. The air got warmer, for which Branwen was grateful, but the walls became closer and the ceiling lower, forcing them to crouch in spots to get through, which made her shiver for different reasons. Unlike Irdina, who hated heights, Branwen had a deep fear of closed spaces. She grasped the skirt of Irdina's long coat and tried not to hold her breath.

There were two more forks in the tunnel, and one three-way split. Each time, Irdina went right, taking them further down, till even she felt her sister's claustrophobia. And then the tunnel ended in a squared stone wall.

"Shit," Irdina whispered. "Fuck, fuck, fuck."

"What now?" Branwen asked, panic creeping into her voice.

"I don't know. Rhona didn't say. Maybe we missed a turn somewhere?" She ran the evenlamp crystal around the square edges of the mortared wall. "This looks like it was a door. Maybe it's been walled in?"

"Wait," Branwen said, her voice steady once more. "Remember Allaigna telling us about the secret door?"

"The one she found when she was a page here?" Irdina and Branwen were only nine when Allaigna had ended her service as a page at the Bastion in disgrace.

Branwen nodded, and pushed past Irdina, pulling out her new folding knife. "Look, there's no mortar here." She ran the knife tip along the top of the wall, then followed it down the edge of the top stone, then in, down, out, and down; in, down, out, and down, tracing a crenellated pattern where the stones interlaced.

"So the wall is removable," said Irdina. "Gimme that." She tapped the stones with Branwen's knife handle, but they gave no different sound no matter where she hit.

"Too thick to sound hollow," mused Branwen.

Irdina's irritation at Rhona, and at herself, for leading them to a dead end grew. She gave the wall a trial push.

"We don't know that it opens outward," said Branwen.

"Well, if it opens inward, we're fucked," snarled Irdina, throwing her shoulder against it.

It moved, but not outward.

"Look," said Branwen, as Irdina stood back, rubbing her shoulder. "This gap is larger."

There was now a visible dark gap where Branwen had run her knife—big enough for Irdina to press the very tips of her fingers into. She reached into the purse inside her waistband and pulled out a hooked piece of metal a handspan long.

"Why are you carrying a hoof-pick?" asked Branwen.

Irdina shrugged. "You never know when you might need one." She pushed the end of the pick into the space between stones and levered the handle back, pushing the stones farther apart.

Branwen slid her fingers into the gap, and Irdina replaced the pick with her own hands. With Irdina pushing and Branwen pulling, the section of masonry lurched and then slid open a handspan, revealing a metal track beneath it, rusty and dirt-filled, and a zigzag gap where the staggered stones separated. Branwen took the towel from her head, looped it around one of the stones, and pulled, while Irdina put her shoulder against the towel's padding. Heaving like draught horses, they coaxed the stones apart.

Branwen looked at Irdina. "How did Allaigna manage this on her own when she was half our size?"

Irdina shrugged. "Maybe it was in better shape?" She took Branwen's towel and used it to clean the dirt from the metal track before Branwen could protest.

Grumbling, Branwen took a tiny jar from her pocket, stuck a finger in it, and rubbed grease along the metal track. "Gimme that," she said, snatching the filthy towel back to wipe off her finger.

Irdina sniffed the air. "Why do you have balsam ointment in your pocket?"

"You never know when you might need it."

They wriggled through the gap and into the space between the inner and outer wall. It was filled with rubble to their left, but to the right a rough path led slightly upwards. Overhead, thick beams, ancient by the look of them, held up planks above their heads.

Irdina lifted the evenlamp, staring at the cobwebbed ceiling. The gaps between planks were just large enough to show the rough stone infill. "How old do you think this wood is?" she asked.

Branwen shuddered, thinking of the weight of rubble above their heads. "Too old. Let's not waste time."

A dozen paces uphill and the path ended at another masonry wall, with another set of zigzag gaps to pry open, and a breath of cold, fresh air when they did.

Irdina pocketed the evenlamp crystal and crawled out under a natural rock overhang in the Bastion's foot, lit by the half moon.

"This seems like a bit of a security flaw," Branwen said, brushing cobwebs and dust from her clothes and shaking out her still-wet hair. The icy air was shocking, but she welcomed it after the terrifying closeness of the tunnels.

Irdina shook her head. "Glaignen said the spring provided protection—that none but Brandis's line could pass through it, or something."

"That sounds fanciful. And like wishful thinking."

"And yet, the Bastion still stands, with Brandis's descendent in its seat."

Branwen had to concede the spring held powerful arcana. She touched her chin, amazed at the absence of the Mageguard's mark that had haunted her these past weeks. "We could just go," she said. "Get on a ship back to Teillai. We've given Grandpapa half the salts we have. Do you think we could trust Rhona with the rest? We could tell Angeley in person what we've found out about Gwannyn."

And see Mama, Irdina thought. She felt the pull of home like the tug of a horse heading for pasture. But she never let a horse win that fight. "We said we'd do this." She planted her heels, anchoring herself to the task.

Branwen nodded, oddly relieved at her sister's stubbornness, and scanned the frosty, moonlit commons that spread out before them. There was only one van camped there, with a pair of piebald draughts hobbled nearby. They picked up their heads to watch the girls approach.

Branwen reached into her jacket and pulled out the letter she'd penned.

The short-grazed commons crunched beneath their feet as they walked toward the wagon-house. A cloaked and hooded figure was sitting on the wagon's back step.

"Glaignen?" Irdina whispered.

The figure pulled back the hood, revealing a cloud of silver hair that caught the moonlight. "Glaignen's asleep, as all young people should be at this hour," said Nourd, standing. "The dead hours of the night are for the old to keep watch." Her occluded gaze was level with theirs, even though she stood on the bottom step. "You came with a message?"

Branwen proffered the note, then hesitated. Nourd most likely couldn't read with her clouded eyes.

"For Irdaign," said Irdina, her grandmother's real name still awkward in her mouth.

Nourd put her hand out, and Branwen placed the letter in it. "Shall I read it aloud?" Branwen asked.

Nourd closed her eyes and held the folded paper to her lips. She recited the message, almost word for word, finishing with, "I will scry Irdaign later this morning. Teillai's sunrise is ahead of ours, but the cocks have not started their calls there either." She opened her eyes, milky in the moonlight. "Unless you would speak to her yourselves."

The sisters looked at one another, feeling the call to home drag at them. Branwen's head moved so slightly only a sister would see it, and Irdina turned to look at Nourd.

"Thank you, grandmother," Irdina said, using the Leisanmira honorific. "But no. Please give her our message … and our love." That felt awkward but important.

"We should get back. The cooks will be up soon, and it's a long way through the rock," Branwen said, though she'd rather go anywhere than back in those tunnels.

The moon was gone by the time they emerged, damp and chilly, into the kitchen garden once more. A single lamp shone from the kitchen windows, and tendrils of smoke from the chimney showed that the first of the ovens was lit, despite the sky's starred blackness. The glass house warmed them temporarily but made them feel all the colder when they stepped outside to the inner courtyard.

As they approached the intersection of the colonnades, a shadow detached itself from the wall: tall and clad in Mageguard black.

"And where have you girls been?" asked Kolluk'khan, her amber eyes and white teeth the only part of her visible in the shadowed corridor.

Branwen tipped her head to one side, a smile creeping onto her normally serious mouth. "I don't think we need to answer that."

"The safety of the royal family is my concern. And that includes you," said the Mageguard, reaching a too-familiar hand toward Branwen.

Irdina stepped between them and put her hand behind her for Branwen to grasp. Kolluk'khan's hand fell on Irdina's shoulder instead, and the mage recoiled as if burned.

"Lucky for you, then," Irdina said. "We are quite safe. I trust you'll see to it we remain so. I think we can agree to stay out of one another's way, yes?"

Branwen couldn't resist a look over her shoulder as they passed the Mageguard. She tapped two fingers on her chin, blissfully free of any arcane mark, and blew a kiss.

§

For more high fantasy, family drama, and political intrigue set in the lands of the Ilmar, check out the spellbinding Allaigna's Song trilogy from JM Landels, and watch for Ilmar Songs, *a collection of short stories due out from Pulp Literature Press in the spring of 2026. pulpliterature.com/allaignas-song/*

THE ARTISTS

Akem
Cover artist, Selfie
Akem is a writer, an illustrator, and an artist in animation. She illustrated *Brown Sugar Babe,* a picture book about the beauty of dark skin, in 2 0 2 0. Her fantasy stories can be found in *Augur Magazine* and *Polar Borealis.* Akem's story 'Shotguns and Jinn' appears in *Pulp Literature* Issue 2 5, and her cover art graces issues 1 6 (*Seabus*), 1 8 (*Windseeker*), and 2 3 (*Greetings*). To see her personal and published artwork, visit akemiart.ca.

Sierra Louie
Illustrator, 'If I Could Hide Away Anywhere'
Sierra Louie is a Vancouver-based cartoonist and editor. Her comics can be found on Instagram @sierralouieart, and her short comic 'Get Home Safe' was published in *Pulp Literature* Issue 4 1, Winter 2 0 2 4. With 'If I Could Hide Away Anywhere', she continues her tradition of drawing tiny bug-like people. Forever inspired by the natural wonders of her childhood, this comic explores Sierra's preoccupation with returning to the earth — in the least morbid way possible, of course. She is currently at work on her first graphic novel, and she would love it if you asked her about it.

Mel Anastasiou

In-house illustrator

Mel Anastasiou loves drawing for *Pulp Literature* because she loves the stories she illustrates. She draws in black and white, working from imagination and inspired by details from Renaissance compositions. You can find illustrations, writing tips, and news about her books and novellas at melanastasiou.wordpress.com, and see more of her artwork on Facebook at Bird and Branch Artwork.

Coming soon...
Stella Ryman and the Search for Thelma Hu
by Mel Anastasiou

Available October 2025 from Pulp Literature Press

AT LONG LAST, EVERYONE'S FAVOURITE OCTOGENARIAN
SLEUTH RETURNS TO SOLVE A NEW MYSTERY ...

HALL OF FAME

These are the heroes — the Patrons and Pulp Literati whose monthly support helped bring you this issue. Please lift your glasses and give them a rousing cheer!

The Brewers
Dana Tye Rally

The Innkeepers
Abigail Bruce
Andrea Kepple
David Jensen
Ev Bishop
Gillian Gardiner
Kevin Harris
Lorna Ens
Mark Francis
Richard Ohnemus
Robin McGillveray
Susan Jackson
Kevin S Moul

The Cicerones
Bjarne Hansen
Jennifer Sommersby
Roger & Anne Anastasiou
Zoë Ricard

The Bartenders
Alana Krider
Andrea Kirkham
Anna Belkine
Brighton Hugg
Bryan Moose
Cheryl Andrichuk
Chris Olee
Dave Wayne
Deepthi Atukorala
Dena Linn Chen
Devan Erno
Emmy Bee
Ernst Pulido
Evelyn Ann
Finnian Burnett
Hannah Moor
James Carlino
Jennifer Getsinger
Jillian Shoichet
Kat Hankinson
Kate Johnson
Katherine Derbyshire

kc dyer
Kelsey Brennan
Kim Seary
KT Wagner
Leny Wagner
Lin Richardson
Margot Landels
Margot Spronk
Megan Shaw
Michelle Balfour
Mike Sylvester
Peter Halasz
Rapscallion
Regina Rogers
Richard Gropp
Ron Graves
Scott F Gray
Shannon Saunders
Star
Suzanne Philip
Venasa Simpson

THE REGULARS

Adam Fout
Alice Rhoades
Andy W
BC
Brandi Estey-Burtt
Catherine Levinson
Charity Tahmaseb
Christopher Bridgen
Jenny Blackford
JS Andrew
Marilyn Holt
Marilyn K
Marta Salek
Meredith Frazier
Michelle Robinson
Peter Darbyshire
Rina Piccolo
Vera

If you would like to join the ranks of these worthies, you can become a patron on Patreon at patreon.com/pulplit or join the Pulp Literati through our website at pulpliterature.com/join-pulp-literati.

The Malahat Review

ESSENTIAL POETRY • FICTION • CREATIVE NONFICTION

Novella Prize

PRIZE MONEY
$2000

ENTRY DEADLINE
February 1, 2026

ENTRY FEE
$35

Commit these deadlines to memory

May 1, 2026
Far Horizons Award for Poetry | $1250
One winner gets the prize

August 1, 2026
Constance Rooke
Creative Nonfiction Prize | $1250
One winner takes all

November 1, 2026
Open Season Awards | $6000
Three writers split the winnings

University
of Victoria

malahatreview.ca
malahat@uvic.ca

MARKETPLACE

Books

Advent *by Michael Kamakana* • We thought we knew what the aliens wanted. Think again. pulpliterature.com/advent

Allaigna's Song: Chorale *by JM Landels* The long-awaited conclusion to the bestselling *Allaigna's Song* trilogy. pulpliterature.com/allaignas-song

Barhopping for Astronauts *by Leo X Robertson* • Sci-fi stories of love, loss, and liquor in the void. pulpliterature.com/books/ barhopping-for-astronauts/

The Extra: A Monument Studios Mystery *by Mel Anastasiou* • Extra Frankie Ray gets her big break on the Silver Screen, until murder steals the scene. pulpliterature.com/the-extra

Stella Ryman and the Search for Thelma Hu *by Mel Anastasiou* • Trapped in a down-at-the-heels care home. You'd be cranky too. pulpliterature.com/stella-ryman-and-the-fairmount-manor-mysteries

What the Wind Brings *by Matthew Hughes* • Winner of the 2020 Endeavour Award • pulpliterature.com/ product-category/novels/matthew-hughes

The Writer's Boon Companion *by Mel Anastasiou* • Thirty Days Towards an Extraordinary Volume • pulpliterature.com/subscribe/the-bookstore

Bookstores

Russell Books • 100-747 Fort St, Victoria, BC • russellbooks.com

Western Sky Books • 2132-2850 Shaughnessy St, Port Coquitlam, BC V3C 6K5 • 604-461-5602 store.westernskybooks.com

White Dwarf / Dead Write Books 3715 10th Ave W, Vancouver, BC V6R 2G5 • 604-228-8223 whitedwarf@deadwrite.com

Printing & Publishing

Fraser Printers • Surrey's Quality Printer • fraserprinters.bc.ca

Conferences & Events

When Words Collide • August 2025 Calgary, AB • whenwordscollide.org

Wine Country Writers' Festival • Sep 2025 • winecountrywritersfestival.ca

Surrey International Writers' Conference • 24–26 October 2025 • siwc.ca

Magazines

Amazing Stories • Back in print!
amazingstories.com

Arc Poetry Magazine • Poetry, essays,
interviews, reviews • arcpoetry.ca

EVENT Magazine • Poetry & prose
eventmagazine.ca

Fiddlehead & SCL • Poetry, fiction,
non-fiction • thefiddlehead.ca

Geist • Ideas + Culture • Made in
Canada • geist.com

Literary Review of Canada • Reviews
on everything from policy and politics
to history, biography, and fiction
reviewcanada.ca

Malahat Review • Poetry, fiction,
creative non-fiction • malahatreview.ca

OnSpec • The Canadian magazine of
the fantastic
onspecmag.wordpress.com

Polar Borealis • Paying market for
new Canadian SF&F writers & artists
polarborealis.ca

Prairie Fire • A Canadian magazine
of new writing • prairiefire.ca

Room Magazine • Literature, Art &
Feminism since 1975
roommagazine.com

Spadina Literary Review • An international quarterly based in Toronto
spadinaliteraryreview.com

SubTerrain Magazine • Fiction,
poetry, photography, and graphic
illustration from uprising Canadian,
US, and International writers and
artists • subterrain.ca

Writing Resources

Dreamers Creative Writing
Workshops • residencies • contests &
more • dreamerswriting.com

Federation of BC Writers
Workshops • contests • networking &
more • bcwriters.ca/join-us

CONTESTS

Pulp Literature runs six annual contests for poetry, flash fiction, short stories, and novel first pages. For contest guidelines, prizes, and entry fees, see pulpliterature.com/contests.

The Raven Short Story Contest
Contest opens: 1 September 2025
Deadline: 15 October 2025
Winner notified: 15 November 2025
Winner published: Issue 50, Spring 2026
Prize: $300

The Bumblebee Flash Fiction Contest
Contest opens: 1 January 2026
Deadline: 15 February 2026
Winner notified: 15 March 2026
Winner published: Issue 51, Summer 2026
Prize: $300

The Magpie Award for Poetry
Contest opens: 1 March 2026
Deadline: 15 April 2026
Winner notified: 15 May 2026
Winner published: Issue 52, Autumn 2026
Prize: $500

The Hummingbird Flash Fiction Prize

Contest opens: 1 May 2026

Deadline: 15 June 2026

Winner notified: 15 July 2026

Winner published: Issue 53, Winter 2027

Prize: $300

The Kingfisher Poetry Prize

Contest opens: 1 July 2026

Deadline: 15 August 2026

Winner notified: 15 September 2026

Winner published: Issue 53, Winter 2027

Prize: $300

The First Page Cage

Contest opens: 1 August 2026

Deadline: 15 September 2026

Winner notified: 15 December 2026

Quarter-finalists published online: Autumn 2026

Prize: $300

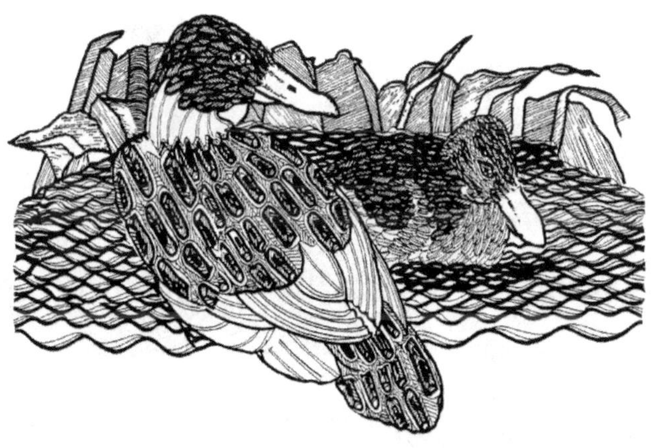

Allaigna's Song
Overture

AMAZON #1 BESTSELLER

JM Land...

Allaigna's Song
Aria

JM Lande...

Allaigna's Song
Chorale

JM Landels

NOW AVAILABLE!

THE MAGICAL CONCLUSION TO THE MUST-READ EPIC TRILOGY

the adventures of Allaigna sing

simply a joy to read

keeps you turning pages from beginning to end

an immensely satisfying epic

PULPLITERATURE.COM/ALLAIGNAS-SONG/

Out of the fires of a Caribbean slave revolt, shipwrecked on the jungle coast of 16th-century Ecuador, an educated slave, a shaman, and a monk hunted by the Inquisition fight for freedom against the might of Imperial Spain.

Dive into an epic slipstream novel of intrigue and adventure from fantasy author Matthew Hughes, the writer George R.R. Martin calls 'criminally underrated,' and Robert J. Sawyer says is 'a towering talent.'

'A triumph!' - Cecelia Holland
'Sensational' - Candas Jane Dorsey

pulpliterature.com
Fantastic Fresh Fiction!

PULP *Literature*

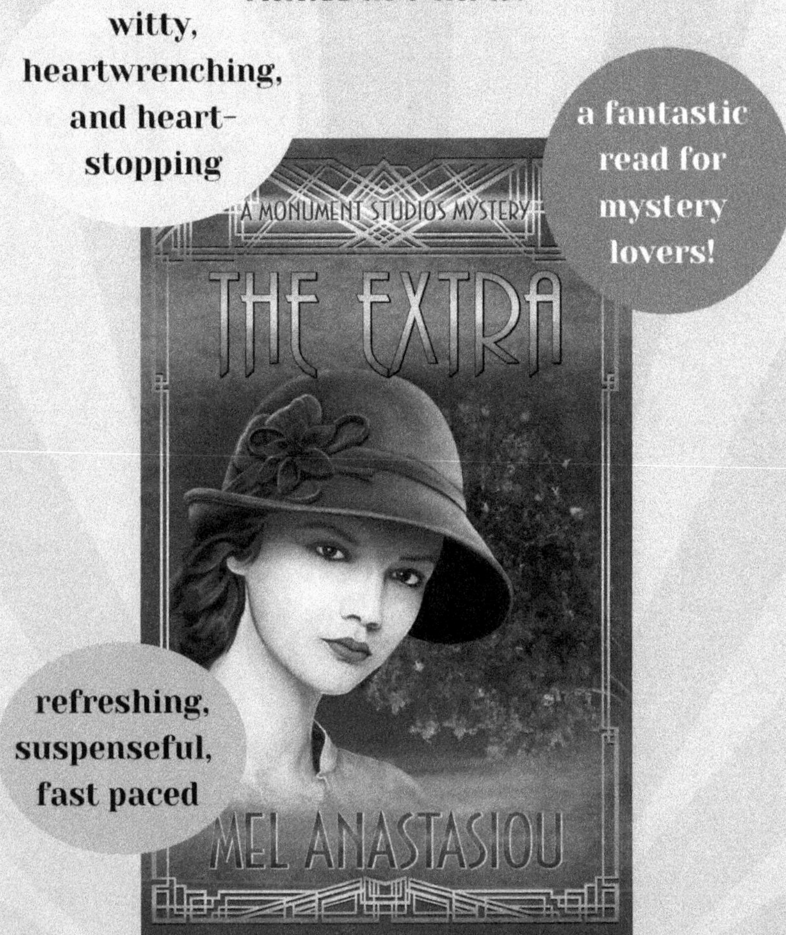

"A DAZZLING SLEUTH OPENS A NEW THRILLER SERIES!"
witty, heartwrenching, and heart-stopping
a fantastic read for mystery lovers!
A MONUMENT STUDIOS MYSTERY
THE EXTRA
refreshing, suspenseful, fast paced
MEL ANASTASIOU
"The conjugal blend of mystery and Hollywood atmosphere works on every level. Very highly recommended."
PULPLITERATURE.COM/THE-EXTRA-A-MONUMENT-STUDIOS-MYSTERY

become our
2,000TH MEMBER!

The Federation of BC Writers is on the brink of reaching an incredible milestone. Soon, we'll be 2,000 members strong!

To celebrate, we're gifting the 2,000th member of our literary community a free pass to an upcoming Writing Intensive of their choice.

Plus, the member who refers the 2,000th registrant will also enjoy a free spot in a Writing Intensive.

Join us and reap the myriad benefits of a FBCW membership. For a complete list, visit:
bcwriters.ca/benefits

ARC **POETRY**

Canada's poetry magazine for over 45 years

3 issues per year, in
Spring, Summer,
and Fall
$40 for one year
$65 for two years*
subscribe online at
arcpoetry.ca

*Subscription rates listed for Canadian subscribers

 @ Arc Poetry Magazine  @ arcpoetrymag

Become a Patron of *Pulp Literature*

By supporting **Pulp Literature** on Patreon with $2 or more per month, you will be laying the foundation for a secure future for the magazine, as well as ensuring that you never miss an issue! Your subscription includes four big issues of short stories, novellas, poetry, comics, and novel excerpts, delivered to your door or electronic mailbox each year. Find us at **patreon.com/pulplit**.

If you prefer to subscribe through our website, go to pulpliterature. com/subscribe.

Or you can send a cheque with the form below to *Subscriptions, Pulp Literature Press, 21955 16 Ave, Langley BC, V2Z 1K5, Canada*

- -

- ❑ **Send me 2 years (8 issues) at the special rate of $110** (save $34)*
- ❑ **Send me 1 year (4 issues) for $60** (save $12)*
- ❑ **Send me 2 years of digital issues for $35** (save $12.92)
- ❑ **Send me 1 year of digital issues for $20** (save $3.96)

Name: ____

Address: ____

City: ________________________________ Prov. / State: _________

Postal code: _____________ Country:_______________________

Email: ____

❑	Payment enclosed	Make cheques payable in Canadian funds to Pulp Literature Press. Include email address for digital editions and Paypal billing, or subscribe at www.pulpliterature.com/subscribe.
❑	Bill me	
❑	New	*for postage outside Canada add $20 per year in North America or $32 per year overseas.
❑	Renewal	

www.ingramcontent.com/pod-product-compliance
Lightning Source LLC
Chambersburg PA
CBHW070652010826
48975CB00013B/977